傲慢與偏見

PRIDE AND PREJUDICE

偏見

Jane Austen

原著 _ Jane Austen

改寫 _ Elspeth Rawstron

譯者 _ 盧相如

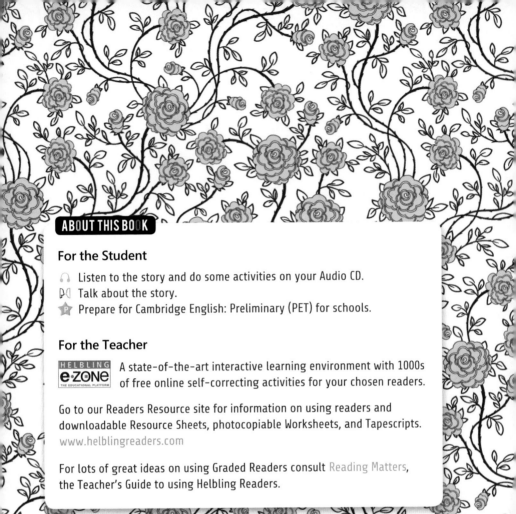

ABOUT THIS BOOK

For the Student

- Listen to the story and do some activities on your Audio CD.
- Talk about the story.
- Prepare for Cambridge English: Preliminary (PET) for schools.

For the Teacher

HELBLING e·ZONE THE EDUCATIONAL PLATFORM — A state-of-the-art interactive learning environment with 1000s of free online self-correcting activities for your chosen readers.

Go to our Readers Resource site for information on using readers and downloadable Resource Sheets, photocopiable Worksheets, and Tapescripts.
www.helblingreaders.com

For lots of great ideas on using Graded Readers consult Reading Matters, the Teacher's Guide to using Helbling Readers.

Level 5 Structures

Modal verb would	Non-defining relative clauses
I'd love to . . .	Present perfect continuous
Future continuous	Used to / would
Present perfect future	Used to / used to doing
Reported speech / verbs / questions	Second conditional
Past perfect	Expressing wishes and regrets
Defining relative clauses	

Structures from other levels are also included.

CONTENTS

About the Author   4
About the Book   6
Before Reading   8

Chapter 1   15
Chapter 2   17
Chapter 3   21
Chapter 4   25
Chapter 5   29
Chapter 6   34
Chapter 7   39
Chapter 8   44
Chapter 9   47

Chapter 10   52
Chapter 11   57
Chapter 12   66
Chapter 13   69
Chapter 14   74
Chapter 15   77
Chapter 16   80
Chapter 17   85
Chapter 18   91

After Reading   94
Test   104
Project Work   106
Translation   108
Answer Key   140

Jane Austen was born in December 1775. Her father was George Austen, a vicar[1] and her mother was called Cassandra. She had seven brothers and sisters, and she was the second youngest. The Austens lived in Steventon in Hampshire, and they were a happy, well-educated and affectionate[2] family. Jane and her sister, called Cassandra like her mother, were very close, and much of what we know about Jane Austen comes from her letters to Cassandra.

Jane Austen began to write stories and sketches for her family when she was twelve years old. When she was a teenager, she was determined[3] to be a published author.

In all her novels, Jane Austen wrote about marriage, but she never married herself. Around Jane's twentieth birthday, she fell in love with Tom Lefroy, a young law student. They met when he was visiting relatives[4] in Hampshire. During his short visit, they spent a lot of time together but his family did not allow them to be together because Jane was not from a wealthy[5] family. He went back to London to study, and two years later, he married the sister of a fellow student.

Jane Austen wrote her six great novels in seven years. *Sense and Sensibility* in 1811; *Pride and Prejudice* in 1813; *Mansfield Park* in 1814; *Northanger Abbey* and *Persuasion*, were published in 1817 after her death. They were all published anonymously[6], but it became known that she was the author. In 1816, Jane became ill. She traveled to Winchester to see a doctor, and she died there on the 18th July 1817. She is buried at Winchester Cathedral.

1 vicar [ˋvɪkɚ] (n.)（英國國教）教區牧師
2 affectionate [əˋfɛkʃənɪt] (a.) 溫柔親切的
3 determined [dɪˋtɝmɪnd] (a.) 已下決心的
4 relative [ˋrɛlətɪv] (n.) 親戚
5 wealthy [ˋwɛlθɪ] (a.) 富有的
6 anonymously [əˋnɑnəməslɪ] (adv.) 匿名地

Pride and Prejudice was first written between October
1796 and August 1797 and it was called *First Impressions*. It
wasn't published, however, until 1813. It was Jane Austen's
second novel. She was twenty-one years old when she first
wrote it. It is still one of the most popular novels in English
literature and it has sold more than 20 million copies.
Pride and Prejudice was published anonymously and was
credited[1] to the author of *Sense and Sensibility*.

Pride and Prejudice is a story of life and love in England
in the 1800s. The story is about Mr. and Mrs. Bennet
and their five unmarried daughters. Mrs. Bennet's main

---

1 credit [ˈkrɛdɪt] (v.) 把……歸於
2 purpose [ˈpɝpəs] (n.) 目的
3 witty [ˈwɪtɪ] (a.) 機智的；詼諧的
4 pride [praɪd] (n.) 驕傲
5 prejudice [ˈprɛdʒədɪs] (n.) 偏見
6 confess [kənˈfɛs] (v.) 坦承
7 delightful [dɪˈlaɪtfəl] (a.) 令人愉快的
8 creature [ˈkritʃɚ] (n.) 生物；產物
9 tolerate [ˈtɑləˌret] (v.) 容忍；寬恕

purpose[2] in life is to see her five daughters married. Consequently, she is very happy when a handsome rich gentleman arrives in the neighborhood, and he falls in love with her eldest daughter Jane. However, when her sister, the clever and witty[3] Elizabeth Bennet first meets his handsome and wealthier friend, Mr. Darcy, she dislikes him. And that is the beginning of their wonderful love story. In order for them to fall in love, his pride[4] and her prejudice[5] must be overcome. About Elizabeth, Jane Austen wrote in a letter:

"I must confess[6] that I think her as delightful[7] a creature[8] as ever appeared in print, and how I shall be able to tolerate[9] those who do not like her at least I do not know."

1 What do you know about the novel *Pride and Prejudice*?
Tick (√) true (T) or false (F).

T	F		
T	F	a	The novel is a romance.
T	F	b	The story takes place in Paris.
T	F	c	It was first published in 1913.
T	F	d	*Pride and Prejudice* was the author's first novel.
T	F	e	The author was a woman.
T	F	f	The central theme of the novel is love and marriage.

2 These things are often found in Jane Austen's novels.
Match them to the pictures.

1. vicar   4. estate
2. housekeeper   5. ball
3. officer   6. carriage

3 Read the passage and then answer the questions.

Mr. Darcy was the main topic of conversation. "Mrs. Long told me that he sat next to her for half an hour without speaking," said Mrs. Bennet.

"Miss Bingley told me," said Jane, "that he never speaks much, unless with his close friends. With *them* he's very friendly."

"I don't believe a word of it, my dear. Everybody says he's very proud," said Mrs. Bennet.

"I don't mind him not talking to Mrs. Long," said Charlotte, "but I mind him not dancing with Elizabeth."

"Another time, Lizzy," said her mother, "don't dance with *him*."

"I think, I can promise never to dance with him," said Elizabeth.

"His pride," said Charlotte Lucas, "doesn't upset *me*. You can't blame a wealthy man, from a good family for being proud."

"That's very true," replied Elizabeth, "and I could easily forgive *his* pride, if he hadn't insulted *mine*."

"Pride," said Mary, "is a very common weakness.

There are very few of us who don't feel pride over one thing or another."

<table>
<tr><td>a</td><td>When is Mr. Darcy friendly?</td></tr>
</table>

(a) When is Mr. Darcy friendly?

(b) How has Mr. Darcy upset Charlotte?

(c) What does Charlotte think about Mr. Darcy's pride? Tick (√).

    ____ (1) She doesn't think he has anything to be proud about.

    ____ (2) She feels he has a right to be proud.

(d) What does Elizabeth promise? Do you think she will keep her promise?

(e) There are two very different opinions of Mr. Darcy in the dialogue. What are they?

4 Read the descriptions of the characters. Try and guess which man each of the Bennet sisters will marry.

Jane Bennet

She is the eldest and the most beautiful of all the Bennet sisters. She is modest, generous and kind and she sees the good in everybody. She is the first of the sisters to fall in love, but she nearly loses the man she loves because she doesn't show that she loves him.

Elizabeth Bennet

She is the second-eldest sister, and she is her father's favorite daughter. She has dark hair and dark brown eyes. She is considered pretty but it is her character that attracts her husband in the end. She is intelligent and witty and she is very independent. She believes that she is a good judge of character but she finds out that she isn't.

Lydia Bennet

She is the youngest of the five sisters, and she is her mother's favorite daughter. She is in fact a younger version of her mother. In the story, she is sixteen years old, and she is silly and romantic. Her parents give her too much freedom. She is very loud and very confident. Her one wish in life is to meet and marry a handsome young officer.

Mr. Bingley

He is good-looking and wealthy. He is also very kind and generous. He never says a bad word about anyone and he defends the Bennet sisters when his own sisters criticize them. He doesn't care that the girl he loves isn't from a wealthy family. He is happy to marry for love.

Mr. Wickham

He is a friendly, charming, good-looking young officer. He charms all the ladies with his good looks, his stylish uniform and his friendly personality. He has no money himself, and his one wish in life is to marry a wealthy girl.

Mr. Darcy

He is very wealthy and good-looking and he is proud of his family's beautiful house and high position in society. He believes that you should marry someone from the same social class. He is shy, and at first he appears arrogant and proud. He doesn't find it easy to talk to people.

5 Underline all the adjectives used in Exercise **4**.
Then look for the adjectives which mean the following
to complete the table.

amuses people and says things people find funny	
thinks often about love	
is able to make everybody like him/her	
isn't proud	
is rich	

6 These verbs are from the story.
Match them with their meanings.

1 look quickly at
2 say something bad about someone
3 look hard at
4 talk
5 say no
6 not take any notice of
7 make fun of
8 go red with embarrassment
9 make someone unhappy by not doing something

_____ a tease

_____ b disappoint

_____ c glance

_____ d blush

_____ e stare

_____ f insult

_____ g chat

_____ h ignore

_____ i refuse

Chapter 1

Everybody knows, that a single man with a large **fortune**[1], must want a wife.

When he first comes to a neighborhood, this truth is **fixed**[2] in the minds of all the neighboring families. He will one day belong to one of their daughters.

"My dear Mr. Bennet," his wife said one morning, "have you heard that Netherfield Park has been **rented**[3] at last?"

"No," replied Mr. Bennet.

"Do you not want to know who's renting it?" cried his wife.

"No, but *you* want to tell me," replied Mr. Bennet.

"A rich young man has rented Netherfield."

"What's his name?"

"Mr. Bingley."

"Is he married or single?"

"Single, of course! A single man with a large fortune, an **income**[4] of four or five thousand pounds a year. Isn't that wonderful for our girls?"

"How can it **affect**[5] them?"

"How can you be so annoying?" replied his wife. "You must know that I'm thinking of him marrying one of them."

---

1 fortune ['fɔrtʃən] (n.) 財富
2 fixed [fɪkst] (a.) 固定的
3 rent [rɛnt] (v.) 租出
4 income ['ɪn,kʌm] (n.) 收入
5 affect [ə'fɛkt] (v.) 影響

"Is that the reason he's coming here?"

"Of course not. But he *might* fall in love with one of them, and that is why you must visit him."

"I see no reason to do that."

"But, my dear, think of your daughters," said Mrs. Bennet.

"I don't need to visit. I'll send him a note telling him he can marry **whichever**[1] daughter he chooses."

"Mr. Bennet, you love **teasing**[2] me," said his wife.

"I hope you'll live to see many rich, young men come into the neighborhood."

"It will be no use to us, if twenty men come, since you won't visit them."

"When there are twenty, I'll visit them all."

Mr. Bennet had **a sense of humor**[3], which after twenty-three years of marriage, his wife still didn't understand. *She* was less difficult to understand. The business of her life was to help her daughters marry.

Mr. Bennet was, in fact, one of the first to visit Mr. Bingley, and he promised to introduce his wife and daughters to him at the next **ball**[4] in two weeks' time.

Mr. and Mrs. Bennet

- How are they different?
- Which of the two characters do you prefer and why?
- Do you know anyone who has been married for 23 years?
- How do they talk to each other?

Chapter 2

🎧 4 The evening of the ball arrived. Mr. Bingley came with his two sisters and another young man.

Mr. Bingley was good-looking, friendly and polite[5]. His sisters were fashionable young women. His friend, Mr. Darcy, soon drew[6] everybody's attention. He was tall, handsome and he had an income of ten thousand pounds[7] a year. The ladies decided he was much more handsome than Mr. Bingley. He was looked at with great admiration[8] for about half the evening, until he was discovered to be proud. Then, neither his wealth[9] nor his large house could save him from having a very unpleasant face.

Mr. Bingley was friendly, danced every dance, was upset[10] that the ball finished so early, and talked of giving one himself at Netherfield. How different he was from his friend! Mr. Darcy only danced with Mr. Bingley's sisters. He refused[11] to be introduced to any other lady. It was decided that he was the proudest, most unpleasant man in the world.

---

1 whichever [hwɪtʃˋɛvɚ] (pron.) 無論哪個
2 tease [tiz] (v.) 戲弄；取笑
3 a sense of humor 幽默感
4 ball [bɔl] (n.) 大型舞會
5 polite [pəˋlaɪt] (a.) 禮貌的；斯文的
6 draw [drɔ] (v.) 吸引
   （動詞三態：draw; drew; drawn）
7 pound [paʊnd] (n.) 英鎊
8 admiration [͵ædməˋreʃən] (n.) 欽佩；讚美
9 wealth [wɛlθ] (n.) 財富
10 upset [ʌpˋsɛt] (v.) 使心煩
   （動詞三態：upset; upset; upset）
11 refuse [rɪˋfjuz] (v.) 拒絕

Everybody disliked him. Mrs. Bennet disliked him even more after he insulted[1] her daughter, Elizabeth.

For two dances, Elizabeth Bennet had no dance partner, and at the time, she overheard[2] a conversation between Mr. Darcy and Mr. Bingley.

"Come on, Darcy," said Mr. Bingley. "You must have a dance."

"You know I hate dancing, unless I know my partner really well. Your sisters are already dancing, and there isn't another girl in the room nice enough to dance with."

"I can't agree with you," cried Mr. Bingley, "I've never met so many pleasant girls, and several of them are very pretty."

"You're dancing with the only beautiful girl in the room," said Mr. Darcy, looking at the eldest Miss Bennet.

"Oh, Jane's the most beautiful girl I've ever seen!" said Mr. Bingley. "But one of her sisters is very pretty."

"Which do you mean?" asked Mr. Darcy, turning and looking for a moment at Elizabeth.

Then he turned away and coldly said, "She's alright, but not beautiful enough to tempt[3] *me*. I'm not in the mood[4] to dance with young ladies who are rejected[5] by other men. You'd better go back to Jane. You're wasting your time with me."

Mr. Bingley followed his advice, and Mr. Darcy walked off.

Elizabeth was upset. However, she had a lively sense of humor, so she jokingly[6] told the story to her friends.

---

1 insult [ɪnˈsʌlt] (v.) 羞辱
2 overhear [ˌovɚˈhɪr] (v.) 無意中聽到；偷聽（動詞三態：overhear; overheard; overheard）
3 tempt [tɛmpt] (v.) 吸引；打動
4 in the mood 有做某事物的心思或興致
5 reject [rɪˈdʒɛkt] (v.) 拒絕
6 jokingly [ˈdʒokɪŋlɪ] (adv.) 打趣地

The whole family enjoyed the ball. Mrs. Bennet was happy that Mr. Bingley danced with Jane twice. Jane was as happy as her mother about this, and Elizabeth was happy for Jane. The younger sisters, Kitty, Mary and Lydia were never without dance partners, which was all they cared about. They all returned home, very happy.

That night, when Jane and Elizabeth were alone, Jane told her sister that she really liked Mr. Bingley.

"He's kind, friendly, funny and I've never met anybody so cheerful!"

"He's also handsome," replied Elizabeth. "His character[1] is therefore complete[2]."

"I was very flattered[3] that he asked me to dance a second time," said Jane.

"He could see that you were about five times as pretty as every other girl in the room. Well, he certainly is very friendly. I allow you to like him. Everybody is good in your eyes[4]" said Elizabeth.

---

1 character [ˋkærɪktɚ] (n.) 個性；品質
2 complete [kəmˋplit] (a.) 完美的
3 flatter [ˋflætɚ] (v.) 奉承；使高興
4 in one's eyes 在某人看來

The Lucas family lived a short walk from Longbourn, the village where the Bennet family lived. Charlotte, their eldest daughter was Elizabeth's best friend.

The Miss Lucases and the Miss Bennets always met to talk about a ball; and so the following morning the Lucases came to visit. Mr. Darcy was the main topic of conversation.

"Mrs. Long told me that he sat next to her for half an hour without speaking," said Mrs. Bennet.

"Miss Bingley told me," said Jane, "that he never speaks much, unless with his close friends. With *them* he's very friendly."

"I don't believe a word of it, my dear. Everybody says he's very proud," said Mrs. Bennet.

"I don't mind him not talking to Mrs. Long," said Charlotte, "but I mind him not dancing with Elizabeth."

"Another time, Lizzy," said her mother, "don't dance with *him*."

"I think, I can promise *never* to dance with him," said Elizabeth.

"His pride," said Charlotte Lucas, "doesn't upset *me*. You can't blame[1] a wealthy man from a good family for being proud."

"That's very true," replied Elizabeth, "and I could easily forgive *his* pride, if he hadn't insulted *mine*."

"Pride," said Mary, "is a very common weakness[2]. There are very few of us who don't feel pride over one thing or another."

Pride

- Is pride a good thing or a bad thing?
- Is there anything you are proud of?

When Jane and Mr. Bingley were together, everybody could see that he was in love with her, and Elizabeth could see that Jane was falling in love too. However, she felt sure nobody else would notice. Elizabeth mentioned this to her friend, Charlotte.

"If a woman doesn't show her feelings for a man," said Charlotte, "she might lose him. Mr. Bingley definitely[3] likes your sister, but she must give him some encouragement[4]."

"Charlotte's right," thought Elizabeth. "Mr. Bingley might not realize that Jane's in love with him."

---

1 blame [blem] (v.) 責備
2 weakness ['wiknɪs] (n.) 弱點
3 definitely ['dɛfənɪtlɪ] (adv.) 明確地
4 encouragement [ɪn'kɝɪdʒmənt] (n.) 鼓勵

Now, Elizabeth was so busy thinking about Jane, she never imagined that she had an admirer[5] too. At first, Mr. Darcy hadn't even thought she was pretty. But then he began to find her unusually intelligent[6]. He noticed that she had very beautiful dark eyes, and he began to like her sense of humor. To her, he was just the man who didn't think she was beautiful enough to dance with.

Mr. Darcy began to wish to know more about her, and so he began to listen to her conversations with others. Elizabeth first noticed him doing this, one evening at a party at Sir William Lucas's house.

"Why did Mr. Darcy listen to my conversation with Colonel Forster?" Elizabeth asked Charlotte.

"That's a question which only Mr. Darcy can answer," said Charlotte.

"Well, if he does it again, I'll tell him I've noticed him."

Mr. Darcy approached[7] them soon afterwards.

Elizabeth turned to him and said, "Don't you think, Mr. Darcy, that I expressed[8] myself very well just now, when I asked Colonel Forster to have a ball at Meryton?"

"Very well," he replied, "but it's a subject women like talking about."

"You're hard on us[9]," said Elizabeth.

This was leading to[10] an argument[11], so Charlotte quickly changed the subject[12]. "I'm going to play the piano, Lizzy."

5 admirer [əd`maɪrə] (n.) 讚賞者
6 intelligent [ɪn`tɛlədʒənt] (a.) 有才智的
7 approach [ə`protʃ] (v.) 接近
8 express [ɪk`sprɛs] (v.) 表達
9 hard on sb 嚴厲對待
10 lead to . . . 導致……後果
11 argument [`ɑrgjəmənt] (n.) 爭論
12 subject [`sʌbdʒɪkt] (n.) 主題

Lydia and Kitty asked her to play some dance music and people began to dance.

Mr. Darcy stood watching. Sir William Lucas was standing next to him. Elizabeth at that moment walked towards them.

"Mr. Darcy, let me introduce Miss Bennet. She's a very good dance partner," said Sir William.

"I don't want to dance," said Elizabeth.

"But you dance so well, Miss Elizabeth," said Sir William. "And although Mr. Darcy dislikes dancing, he can't have any objection[1] to dancing with you."

Elizabeth raised her eyebrows[2]. "Can't he?" she said and turned away.

Her refusal to dance hadn't harmed[3] her in Mr. Darcy's eyes, and he was thinking happily about her, when Miss Bingley walked over and said, "I can guess the subject of your thoughts."

"I shouldn't think so," he replied.

"You're thinking what a boring evening this is; and I agree with you."

"You're completely wrong. I was thinking what beautiful eyes a certain lady has."

"And which lady is that?" asked Miss Bingley.

"Miss Elizabeth Bennet," replied Mr. Darcy.

1 objection [əbˋdʒɛkʃən] (n.) 反對
2 raise one's eyebrows 感到驚訝而揚眉
3 harm [hɑrm] (v.) 傷害
4 carriage [ˋkærɪdʒ] (n.) 馬車
5 horseback [ˋhɔrsˌbæk] (n.) 馬背
6 delighted [dɪˋlaɪtɪd] (a.) 高興的
7 die of 因……而死亡

Chapter 4

The next day, a note from Netherfield arrived for Miss Bennet.

"Well, Jane, who's it from?" asked her mother.

"It's from Miss Bingley," said Jane. "She's inviting me to dinner. Her brother and Mr. Darcy will be dining out."

"Dining out," said Mrs. Bennet, "that's very unlucky."

"Can I have the carriage[4]?" asked Jane.

"No, my dear, you should go on horseback[5], because it might rain. Then you'll have to stay all night," said her mother.

Jane went on horseback, and it began to rain heavily. Jane's sisters were worried about her, but her mother was delighted[6]. The rain continued all evening. Jane couldn't come home.

"That was a lucky idea of mine!" said Mrs. Bennet.

The next morning, however, Elizabeth received a note.

"Jane's caught a terrible cold. I must go there at once," cried Elizabeth.

"Well, my dear," said Mr. Bennet, "if your daughter dies, it will be a comfort to know that it was all for Mr. Bingley."

"People don't die of[7] colds," said Mrs. Bennet.

Elizabeth, however, really wanted to see Jane, so she walked to Netherfield to see her.

When she arrived, she was shown into the breakfast room, and was politely welcomed by Mr. Bingley and his two sisters.

Jane was very ill, so Elizabeth went up to see her immediately.

At three o'clock, Elizabeth had to leave, but Jane didn't want her to go.

Miss Bingley invited her to stay at Netherfield, and a servant was sent to Longbourn to tell the family and bring back some clothes.

At half-past six, Elizabeth went down for dinner. Jane was not better, and Mr. Bingley was very worried about her.

When dinner was over, Elizabeth went to sit with Jane again, and Miss Bingley began criticizing[1] her as soon as she left the room.

"She has no manners[2], no conversation, no style, no beauty."

Her sister, Mrs. Hurst thought the same, and added, "I'll never forget her appearance this morning. She looked very wild."

"She did, Louisa. Her hair was so untidy!"

"Yes, and her dress was covered in mud[3]."

"I thought Miss Elizabeth Bennet looked very well this morning," said Mr. Bingley. "I didn't notice her dirty dress."

"*You* noticed it, Mr. Darcy, I'm sure," said Miss Bingley. "I'm afraid that this adventure has affected your admiration of her beautiful eyes."

"Not at all," he replied; "they were brightened[4] by the exercise."

---

1 criticize [ˈkrɪtɪ͵saɪz] (v.) 批評;評論
2 manners [ˈmænəz] (n.) 禮貌;規矩
3 mud [mʌd] (n.) 泥巴
4 brighten [ˈbraɪtn̩] (v.) 使明亮

A short pause followed.

"Miss Jane Bennet is a very sweet girl, and I really wish she were well married," said Mrs. Hurst. "But with such a father and mother, I'm afraid there's no chance of that."

"I think you said that their uncle is a lawyer in Meryton," said Miss Bingley.

"Yes, and they have another uncle, who lives somewhere near Cheapside[1] in London."

"How awful," said her sister, and they both laughed.

"If they had enough uncles to fill *all* Cheapside," cried Mr. Bingley, "it wouldn't make them one bit less charming."

"But it must reduce[2] their chance of marrying well," replied Mr. Darcy.

Mr. Bingley didn't reply, but his sisters agreed.

Criticism

- What do Miss Bingley and Mrs. Hurst criticize about Elizabeth?
- What does it show about their characters?

1 Cheapside ['tʃip,saɪd] (n.) 倫敦的齊普賽街（非時尚區）
2 reduce [rɪ'djus] (v.) 減少
3 amuse [ə'mjuz] (v.) 消遣
4 frequently ['frikwəntlɪ] (adv.) 頻繁地

Chapter 5

(14)   The next evening, Elizabeth joined the party in the living room. Mr. Darcy was writing a letter, and Miss Bingley was sitting near him, watching him. Elizabeth amused[3] herself by listening to their conversation.

"What beautiful handwriting you have," said Miss Bingley.

Mr. Darcy said nothing.

"How happy Miss Darcy will be to receive such a letter!" said Miss Bingley.

He didn't reply.

"Please tell your sister that I'd love to see her."

"I've already told her that once."

"Do you always write such charming long letters to her, Mr. Darcy?"

"They're generally long but whether always charming I don't know," he said finishing his letter and putting down his pen.

Then, he asked Miss Bingley to play something on the piano. Miss Bingley moved quickly to the piano and sat down.

While she was playing, Elizabeth couldn't help noticing, how frequently[4] Mr. Darcy's eyes were fixed on her. It was very strange. It couldn't possibly be because he liked her. In the end, she decided he had seen some fault in her. The idea didn't upset her. She liked him too little.

(15) Mr. Darcy, however, had never been so **attracted**[1] to a woman as he was to Elizabeth. He really felt, that if she were from a good family, he would be in danger of falling in love with her.

Miss Bingley was jealous. She hoped Jane would **recover**[2] quickly and then Elizabeth could go home.

After dinner, Jane came to sit in the living room. Mr. Bingley was happy. He sat down by her, and he hardly talked to anybody else. Elizabeth watched them delighted.

When tea was over, Mr. Darcy picked up a book. Miss Bingley did the same, but she wasn't interested in reading it. She had only chosen the book because it was the second volume of Mr. Darcy's book.

She looked round the room in search of other **entertainment**[3]. On hearing her brother talking about a ball to Jane, she turned to him and asked, "Are you serious about having a ball at Netherfield? I think you should ask everybody here first. Not everybody likes balls. "

"If you mean Darcy," cried her brother, "he can go to bed before the ball begins. We're having a ball and that's final."

Miss Bingley didn't answer, and soon afterwards she got up and walked about the room. Mr. Darcy continued to read his book. She made one final **effort**[4] to get his attention.

"Elizabeth," she said, "come and walk around the room with me."

---

1 attract [ə`trækt] (v.) 吸引
2 recover [rɪ`kʌvɚ] (v.) 恢復
3 entertainment [ˌɛntɚ`tenmənt] (n.) 餘興；娛樂
4 effort [`ɛfɚt] (n.) 努力

Elizabeth was surprised, but she agreed.

This time, Miss Bingley was successful. Mr. Darcy looked up and closed his book.

Miss Bingley invited him to join them, but he **declined**[1].

"I can only imagine two reasons for you choosing to walk up and down the room together."

"What could he mean?" asked Miss Bingley. "Do you know, Elizabeth?"

"No," said Elizabeth. "But the easiest way to disappoint[2] him is not to ask him for an explanation."

Miss Bingley, however, didn't want to **disappoint** Mr. Darcy, and so she asked him for an explanation.

"Either you have secrets to discuss," said Mr. Darcy, "or you want to **show off**[3] your **figures**[4]. If it's the first, I'll be in your way, and if it's the second, I can admire you much better as I sit by the fire."

"Oh, shocking!" cried Miss Bingley. "How shall we punish him?"

"Nothing's easier, if you really want to," said Elizabeth. "Laugh at him."

"But Mr. Darcy is not a man to be laughed at."

"That's a pity," cried Elizabeth, "for I love to laugh."

"The wisest men might be laughed at by someone who loves to laugh at people," said Mr. Darcy.

(17) "Of course," replied Elizabeth, "but I never laugh at what is wise and good. I only laugh at weaknesses such as **vanity**[5] and pride."

"Vanity is a weakness but pride, pride is always necessary," said Mr. Darcy.

Elizabeth turned away to hide a smile.

"Your examination of Mr. Darcy is over, I think," said Miss Bingley. "And what is the **result**[6]?"

"Mr. Darcy has no faults. He said so himself."

"I've got plenty of faults," said Mr. Darcy. "I can't forgive or forget an **offense**[7] against me. My good opinion once lost, is lost forever."

"That is a fault!" agreed Elizabeth. "But you've chosen your fault well. I can't laugh at it."

"Let's have some music," cried Miss Bingley, tired of a conversation in which she had no share.

The piano was opened, and Mr. Darcy felt **relieved**[8]. He had begun to feel the danger of paying Elizabeth too much attention. She attracted him more than he liked.

Jane and Elizabeth left Netherfield the next day.

---

1 decline [dɪˋklaɪn] (v.) 婉拒;謝絕
2 disappoint [͵dɪsəˋpɔɪnt] (v.) 使失望
3 show off 炫耀
4 figure [ˋfɪgjɚ] (n.) 體態

5 vanity [ˋvænətɪ] (n.) 虛榮
6 result [rɪˋzʌlt] (n.) 結果
7 offense [əˋfɛns] (n.) 冒犯;觸怒
8 relieved [rɪˋlivd] (a.) 放心的

Chapter 6

(18)   After breakfast, one morning, all the sisters walked to
Meryton to visit their uncle.

As they entered the village, their attention was caught by a
handsome young officer, walking with Mr. Denny. Mr. Denny
introduced them to his friend, Mr. Wickham. The whole party
were still standing and talking together, when Mr. Darcy and
Mr. Bingley rode down the street.

On seeing the ladies, the two gentlemen came over to join
them.

"I was on my way to Longbourn to see you," Mr. Bingley said
to Jane.

Mr. Darcy was just deciding not to look at Elizabeth, when
he suddenly noticed Mr. Wickham. Elizabeth saw both their
expressions [1]. Both changed color, one went white, the other
red. What could it mean?

A minute later, Mr. Bingley said his goodbyes and rode on
with his friend.

Mr. Denny and Mr. Wickham walked with the young ladies
to the door of their uncle's house, and then they left.

---

1 expression [ɪk'sprɛʃən] (n.) 表情

(19) As they walked home, Elizabeth told Jane about the
awkwardness[1] between Mr. Darcy and Mr. Wickham.

The next evening, the five sisters dined[2] at their uncle's
house. The girls were all happy to hear that Mr. Wickham and
some other officers from the barracks[3] were coming too. The
best of the officers were at the party.

"But," thought Elizabeth, "Mr. Wickham is more handsome
than them all."

Mr. Wickham was the happy man towards whom every
female[4] eye was turned, and Elizabeth was the happy woman
he finally sat down next to.

Whilst the others played cards, Mr. Wickham talked to
Elizabeth. Elizabeth really wanted to know how he knew Mr.
Darcy. Luckily, Mr. Wickham brought up[5] the subject.

"How long has Mr. Darcy been at Netherfield?" he asked.

"About a month," said Elizabeth. "Do you know him well?"

"Yes," replied Mr. Wickham. "*My* father looked after his
father's estate[6], so we spent a lot of time together when we
were growing up."

Elizabeth looked surprised.

"You may well be surprised, Miss Bennet, after seeing our
meeting yesterday. Do you know Mr. Darcy well?"

"As much as I ever wish to," said Elizabeth. "I think he's very
unpleasant. He isn't liked at all here."

1 awkwardness [ˈɔkwədnəs] (n.) 笨拙
2 dine [daɪn] (v.) 用餐；宴請
3 barrack [ˈbærək] (n.) 兵營
4 female [ˈfimel] (a.) 女（性）的
5 bring up 帶來
6 estate [ɪsˈtet] (n.) 地產；財產

(20) "His father was a very good man and he was very fond of *me*," said Mr. Wickham. "He left me the best vicarage[1] in the county[2] in his will[3]. Darcy gave it to somebody else."

"That's terrible!" cried Elizabeth. "But how could he ignore[4] the will?"

"It was informal, and the fact is, he hates me," said Mr. Wickham.

"But why does he hate you?"

"He was jealous of his father's love for me."

"How strange!" cried Elizabeth.

They continued talking till dinner and then the rest of the ladies had their share of Mr. Wickham's attention. Everybody liked him.

Wickham

- What is Mr. Wickham telling Elizabeth?
- What does Elizabeth think?
- What type of person do you think Wickham is? Why?

1 vicarage [ˈvɪkərɪdʒ] (n.) 牧師住宅或職位
2 county [ˈkaʊntɪ] (n.) 郡；縣
3 will [wɪl] (n.) 遺囑
4 ignore [ɪgˈnor] (v.) 忽視；不理會

5 look forward to 期待
　（後接名詞或動名詞）
6 avoid [əˈvɔɪd] (v.) 避開；避免
7 amaze [əˈmez] (v.) 使吃驚

Chapter 7

(21) The day of the Netherfield ball finally arrived. Jane looked forward to[5] an evening spent with Mr. Bingley, and Elizabeth looked forward to dancing with Mr. Wickham.

As soon as she arrived at Netherfield, Elizabeth looked for Mr. Wickham, but he wasn't there. She asked Mr. Denny.

"Mr. Wickham had to go to town on business," Mr. Denny told Elizabeth. "In my opinion, I think he wanted to avoid[6] Mr. Darcy."

Elizabeth was now sure that Mr. Darcy was responsible for Mr. Wickham's absence. When he came over to greet her, she found it very hard to be polite to him. She also found it difficult to be polite to Mr. Bingley. But Elizabeth wasn't unhappy for long.

After talking to Charlotte Lucas, she felt better. They were laughing together when Mr. Darcy came over and asked Elizabeth to dance. She was so surprised that she accepted him.

And so Elizabeth took her place on the dance floor, amazed[7] that she was standing opposite Mr. Darcy. They stood for a while without speaking. Then, Elizabeth said something about the dance. Mr. Darcy replied, and then he was silent again.

After a pause, she said, "It's *your* turn to say something now, Mr. Darcy. I talked about the dance, and *you* could say something about the size of the room, or the number of couples."

He smiled, and asked, "Do you and your sisters often walk to Meryton?"

"Yes," she answered. "When you saw us there the other day, we had just met Mr. Wickham."

Mr. Darcy's face went red and he frowned[1]. "Mr. Wickham makes friends easily. Whether he can *keep* them, is less certain," he said.

"I hear, he's been unlucky enough to lose *your* friendship," replied Elizabeth.

Mr. Darcy didn't answer. At that moment, Sir William Lucas came over, "You have a lovely partner, Mr. Darcy," he said. "I hope to see you dance together more often, especially when a certain marriage, (glancing[2] at Jane and Bingley) takes place."

Mr. Darcy looked worried by this, and he stared[3] at Mr. Bingley and Jane. Then, he turned to Elizabeth, and said, "I'm sorry, I've forgotten what we were talking about."

"I don't think we were talking at all. We've tried two or three subjects already without success. I've no idea what to talk about now."

"Let's talk about books," said Mr. Darcy, smiling.

"Books! Oh, no, I'm sure we never read the same books, or not with the same feelings."

---

1 frown [fraʊn] (v.) 皺眉　　3 stare [stɛr] (v.) 盯；凝視
2 glance [glæns] (v.) 一瞥

"I'm sorry you think so; but if that's the case, we can compare[1] our different opinions."

"No. I can't talk about books in a ballroom." There was a pause and then Elizabeth said, "I remember you once saying, Mr. Darcy, that you hardly ever forgave. That doesn't happen often, I hope."

"It doesn't," he said.

"And you never allow yourself to be blinded by prejudice?"

"I hope not."

"People who never change their opinion must be very sure of judging properly in the first place," said Elizabeth.

"What's this conversation leading to?" asked Mr. Darcy.

"To *your* character," she said. "I'm trying to understand it."

"And have you been successful?"

She shook her head. "I hear such different things about you. I'm confused[2]"

"I can't believe that," he replied, "and I'd prefer it if you didn't form an opinion of my character just now, because I don't think it'll be correct."

"But I might never have another opportunity," Elizabeth replied.

"I don't want to spoil your fun[3]," he said coldly.

The dance ended and they parted[4] in silence; each of them unhappy. Mr. Darcy, however, had such strong feelings for[5] Elizabeth, he soon forgave her, and he directed all his anger against Mr. Wickham.

(24) Elizabeth turned her attention to a happier subject—her sister and Mr. Bingley. She could now imagine Jane happily married and living in this house. Her mother was thinking the same.

When they sat down to eat something, Elizabeth overheard her mother telling Lady Lucas that Jane would soon be married to Mr. Bingley.

Elizabeth could see that the conversation was overheard by Mr. Darcy and he looked very **disapproving**[6]. Elizabeth was embarrassed. In fact it seemed that her whole family had an agreement to embarrass themselves as much as they could. Her sister Mary **insisted**[7] on singing, even though she **couldn't sing a note in tune**[8], and Kitty and Lydia were very **giggly**[9] and silly.

Elizabeth just wanted to go home, but her mother made sure that the Bennets were the last to leave the ball. Their carriage came a quarter of an hour after everybody else had left.

When at last they stood to leave, Mrs. Bennet asked Mr. Bingley to dine with them at Longbourn.

"Thank you, I'll come as soon as I can," he said, "but tomorrow I have to go to London."

1 compare [kəm`pɛr] (v.) 比較
2 confused [kən`fjuzd] (a.) 搞糊塗了
3 spoil one's fun 弄得掃興
4 part [pɑrt] (v.) 分開
5 have strong feelings for sb 對某人有強烈的感覺、愛意
6 disapprove [ˌdɪsə`pruv] (v.) 不贊成；不同意
7 insist [ɪn`sɪst] (v.) 堅持
8 can't sing a note in tune 唱歌五音不全
9 giggly [`gɪglɪ] (a.) 咯咯傻笑的

Chapter 8

The next day, a letter was delivered[1] to Jane. As Jane read it, Elizabeth could see she was upset. "It's from Caroline Bingley," she said. "They've all left Netherfield. They're on their way to London."

"Don't worry, Jane. Mr. Bingley won't stay in London for long."

"But you don't know the *whole* story yet," said Jane. "Listen to this. Mr. Darcy wants to see his sister; and we really want to see her too. Georgiana Darcy is the most beautiful young lady. Louisa and I hope she might soon be our sister-in-law[2]. My brother really admires her too."

"What do you think of *that*, Lizzy?" asked Jane. "Isn't it clear that Caroline doesn't want me to be her sister-in-law. And she's sure of her brother's indifference[3]."

"I don't agree," said Elizabeth. "Miss Bingley knows that her brother's in love with you, but she wants him to marry Georgiana Darcy."

Jane shook her head.

"You must believe me, Jane. Everybody can see he's in love with you. If Miss Bingley saw half as much love in Mr. Darcy for herself, she'd order her wedding dress[4]."

---

1 deliver [dɪˈlɪvə] (v.) 遞送；發表
2 sister-in-law [ˈsɪstərɪnˌlɔ]
    (n.) 小姑；嫂嫂；弟媳
3 indifference [ɪnˈdɪfərəns]
    (n.) 冷淡；漠不關心
4 wedding dress 婚紗

Marrying Well

- Why does Miss Bingley write this letter to Jane?
- Why does she want her brother to marry Miss Darcy?

"But, Lizzy, how can I be happy, marrying a man whose sisters and friends all want him to marry somebody else?"

"If the unhappiness of upsetting his sisters is stronger than the happiness of being his wife, you shouldn't marry him," said Elizabeth.

"But you know I'd marry him immediately" said Jane, smiling.

"Yes, I do, so I can't feel sorry for you."

That week, their aunt, Mrs. Gardiner invited Jane to stay with her in London and Jane was excited at the thought of seeing Mr. Bingley there. However, a month passed, and Jane didn't see Mr. Bingley at all. All thoughts of marrying him were over and Jane was very unhappy.

1 destined ['dɛstɪnd] (a.) 命中注定的
2 put off 拖延

Chapter 9

(27)   In March, Elizabeth went to stay with her friend, Charlotte, and her new husband, Mr. Collins, at the vicarage on Lady Catherine de Bourgh's estate, Rosings. It was Easter and Lady Catherine's nephew, Mr. Darcy, was coming to visit his aunt. He would be somebody new at Lady Catherine's dinner parties at Rosings.

"And," thought Elizabeth, "it'll be entertaining to see how little chance Miss Bingley has of marrying him. Lady Catherine tells me he's **destined**[2] to marry her daughter."

Mr. Darcy's cousin, Colonel Fitzwilliam, came with him to Rosings. And, to the great surprise of everybody, they came to visit the vicarage.

"I have you to thank for this visit," said Charlotte. "Mr. Darcy would never come so soon to visit me."

After that visit, Elizabeth saw a lot of Mr. Darcy and his cousin at dinner parties and also on her walks through the park. One day, whilst walking through the park, she met Colonel Fitzwilliam. They walked to the vicarage together.

"Are you really leaving Rosings on Saturday?" Elizabeth asked.

"Yes, if Darcy doesn't **put it off**[2] again," replied Colonel Fitzwilliam.

Colonel Fitzwilliam and Elizabeth chatted until they arrived back at the vicarage. During their conversation Elizabeth learnt that Mr. Darcy had saved one of his friends from a bad marriage.

"There were strong objections to the lady's family," Colonel Fitzwilliam told her. Elizabeth was sure that this friend was Mr. Bingley. "I knew it," she thought. "Mr. Darcy has stopped Mr. Bingley from seeing Jane. His pride is the **cause**[1] of all Jane's unhappiness." She felt very angry.

Once back in her room at the vicarage, she cried so much she got a headache. She didn't want to see Mr. Darcy that evening, so she decided not to go to the dinner party at Rosings.

That evening, Elizabeth read through Jane's recent letters again. At least, Mr. Darcy was leaving Rosings soon and in less than a **fortnight**[2] she would be with Jane again.

Suddenly, the door bell rang, and Mr. Darcy walked into the room. Elizabeth was very surprised. Mr. Darcy asked how she was, and she answered him with cold politeness.

He sat down for a few moments, and then he got up and walked about the room. After a silence of several minutes, he said, "I've tried to hide my feelings, but I can't hide them any longer. I love you."

Elizabeth was so **astonished**[3] she couldn't speak. She stared, **blush**ed[4], and was silent.

(29) He was encouraged by her silence, and he told her all that he felt for her. Unfortunately, he didn't only speak of love. He also spoke of her family's **poverty**[5] and low social **position**[6].

"In spite of everything," he said, "I've found it impossible to stop loving you. Will you marry me?"

"He's sure I'll accept his **proposal**[7]," Elizabeth thought. This annoyed her, so she said, "No. I can't marry you."

Proposal

- Did you expect Elizabeth to accept or to refuse?
- What would you do if someone proposed to you in this way?

Mr. Darcy looked surprised. He turned pale, and she could see the hurt in his eyes. He couldn't speak for a while. The silence was awful.

Finally, he said, "I'd like to know why you've rejected me."

"You've just told me you don't *want* to love me. And besides, I can't marry a man who's **destroyed**[8] my sister's happiness," replied Elizabeth.

---

1 cause [kɔz] (n.) 起因
2 fortnight [ˈfɔrnaɪt] (n.) 兩星期
3 astonished [əˈstɑnɪʃt] (a.) 驚訝的
4 blush [blʌʃ] (v.) 臉紅

5 poverty [ˈpɑvɚtɪ] (n.) 貧窮
6 position [pəˈzɪʃən] (n.) 地位
7 proposal [prəˈpozḷ] (n.) 求婚
8 destroy [dɪˈstrɔɪ] (v.) 毀壞；破壞

As she said this, Mr. Darcy changed color.

"You **separated**[1] Jane and Mr. Bingley. Can you **deny**[2] it?" she asked.

"I can't deny it," he said calmly. "Towards *him* I've been kinder than towards myself."

"But this isn't the only reason for my dislike," Elizabeth continued. "You've **ruin**ed[3] Mr. Wickham's life."

"You take a great interest in that gentleman," said Mr. Darcy, upset.

"Anybody who knew his **misfortunes**[4] would feel an interest in him," replied Elizabeth.

"His misfortunes!" said Mr. Darcy **sarcastically**[5]. "Yes, his misfortunes have been great."

"And it's all your fault," cried Elizabeth. "You've made him a poor man."

"And this," cried Mr. Darcy, "is your opinion of me. I know I've hurt your pride, but I'm not **ashamed**[6] of the feelings I've explained to you. Could you expect me to be happy about your family?"

Elizabeth was very angry now, but she tried to speak calmly. "*Nothing* would make me accept your proposal."

Mr. Darcy looked at her with an expression of **disbelief**[7] and embarrassment.

31 She went on, "You're proud and **selfish**[8]. You never think of other people's feelings. After knowing you for a month, I felt that you were the last man in the world that I could marry."

"You've said enough, Madam. I understand your feelings perfectly. Forgive me for taking up so much of your time, and accept my best wishes for your health and happiness." And with these words, he left.

Then, Elizabeth sat down and cried for half an hour. She had received an offer of marriage from Mr. Darcy! He had been in love with her for so many months! So much in love as to wish to marry her in spite of his objections to her family. It was unbelievable! But his pride, his awful pride. His part in Jane's unhappiness, and his cruelty towards Mr. Wickham. No! She could never marry him.

Mr. Darcy

- How do you think Mr. Darcy feels?
- Do you think Elizabeth is right about Mr. Darcy and Mr. Wickham?

---

1 separate ['sɛpə,ret] (v.) 使分散
2 deny [dɪ'naɪ] (v.) 否認
3 ruin ['rʊɪn] (v.) 毀滅
4 misfortune [mɪs'fɔrtʃən] (n.) 不幸
5 sarcastically [sɑr'kæstɪkəlɪ] (adv.) 挖苦地
6 ashamed [ə'ʃemd] (a.) 羞愧的；難為情的
7 disbelief [,dɪsbə'lif] (n.) 不相信；懷疑
8 selfish ['sɛlfɪʃ] (a.) 自私的

The next morning, there was a letter for Elizabeth. It was from Mr. Darcy. Elizabeth opened the letter, and began to read it.

Don't worry, Madam. This letter doesn't contain another marriage proposal. There are some things I need to explain to you.

Last night, you accused[1] me of two things. The first, is that I've separated Mr. Bingley from your sister. The second, is that I've ruined Mr. Wickham's life. I hope that after reading this letter, you'll see that it's not completely my fault. If, in my explanation, I upset you, I'm very sorry.

I watched Bingley and I could see he was falling in love with your sister. In fact I've never seen him so much in love before. I also watched your sister and I could see that she wasn't in love with Bingley. She enjoyed the attention but she had no real feelings for him. He was going to get hurt. If you are really sure of her love for him, then I was wrong. But in my defense, your sister didn't look like a girl who was in love.

(33) I know Bingley wasn't worried about Jane's lack of social position and wealth. But there were other causes for concern[2]. The total lack of good manners shown by your mother, your three younger sisters, and occasionally[3] even by your father. Forgive me. It upsets me to offend[4] you. You and your elder sister Jane can only ever be praised for your behavior. On the evening of the ball, I decided to save my friend from an unhappy marriage.

Then I learnt that his sisters felt the same way. In London, I convinced[5] Bingley that your sister didn't love him. That was the only thing that stopped him from contacting her again. I can't blame myself for doing this. There is just one thing which I'm not happy about. I didn't tell Bingley that your sister was in London. I knew that he still loved her so I couldn't allow them to meet. I did it for the best. I didn't mean to hurt your sister.

Regarding[6] Mr. Wickham, I have to tell you all the facts. After my father's death, Mr. Wickham wrote to inform me that he didn't want to become a vicar. He wanted to study law. I knew he wouldn't make a very good vicar. I agreed to give him three thousand pounds, so he could study law.

---

1 accuse [ə'kjuz] (v.) 指控
2 concern [kən'sɜn] (n.) 擔心的事
3 occasionally [ə'keʒənl̩ɪ] (adv.) 偶爾
4 offend [ə'fɛnd] (v.) 冒犯；觸怒
5 convince [kən'vɪns] (v.) 說服
6 regarding [rɪ'gɑrdɪŋ] (prep.) 關於

However, he didn't really want to study law. When his money ran out, he wrote to me. He told me that he would like to become a vicar after all[1]. Could he now have the vicarage promised to him by my father? I refused him. He was very angry with me. After this, we lost contact. Then last summer he came into my life again.

I must now tell you something which I haven't told anybody else. I'm sure you'll keep this a secret. Last summer, my sister, Georgiana fell in love with him. They planned to elope[2]. She was then only fifteen. Luckily she told me about the elopement, so I stopped it. You can imagine how I felt. Mr. Wickham's main interest in my sister was her fortune, which is thirty thousand pounds.

Now, I hope, you'll no longer accuse me of cruelty towards Mr. Wickham. I know he can be very charming so I don't blame you for believing him. You couldn't know his true character.

Colonel Fitzwilliam will confirm my story.

God bless you.

Fitzwilliam Darcy

---

1 after all 畢竟；終究
2 elope [ɪˋlop] (v.) 私奔
3 grateful [ˋgretfəl] (a.) 感激的
4 compliment [ˋkɑmpləmənt] (n.) 恭維
5 wander [ˋwɑndɚ] (v.) 徘徊；閒逛

(35)   Now Elizabeth understood why Mr. Darcy had broken up the relationship between Jane and Mr. Bingley. He didn't think Jane loved Mr. Bingley. He was right. Jane didn't show her feelings. Hadn't Charlotte said that too?

When she read this account of Mr. Wickham, she felt very upset. Now she could see that Mr. Darcy was not to blame for Mr. Wickham's misfortunes.

Elizabeth began to feel ashamed of herself. "I've been so blind, so prejudiced, so stupid," she cried. "I've prided myself on being a good judge of character but I'm not!"

When she came to the part of the letter about her family, she felt terrible. He was right about that too. Her mother and her sisters' behavior often embarrassed her. She was grateful[3] for the compliment[4] to herself and her sister. She now saw that Jane's disappointment was in fact caused by her own family. This really upset her. She went out for a walk.

After wandering[5] through the park for two hours, thinking about the letter, she returned home. Charlotte immediately told her that Mr. Darcy had called to say goodbye.

For days, the letter from Mr. Darcy filled Elizabeth's thoughts and she wished she could talk to Jane about it.

Talk

- Do you think it is important to talk to someone about your thoughts?
- Who do you normally talk to?

Finally, her visit to the vicarage came to an end, and she returned to Longbourn.

As soon as she arrived, Elizabeth told Jane about Mr. Darcy's proposal. Jane was astonished.

"Do you think I should have accepted him?" asked Elizabeth.

"Oh, no," said Jane. "But poor Mr. Darcy!"

"Oh, Jane, I was really vain[1] and prejudiced and stupid!"

"How unfortunate[2] that you let Mr. Darcy see how prejudiced you were," said Jane.

"I know. I was really rude[3] to him. And now there's one thing I'd like your advice on. Should we tell our friends about Mr. Wickham?"

"I don't think we need to," said Jane.

"I agree," said Elizabeth. "Mr. Wickham's regiment[4] is moving to Brighton; so he'll be gone soon."

Elizabeth felt better after this conversation. "I've told Jane two of the secrets. But I can't tell her that Mr. Bingley loves her. He must tell her that himself."

Now she was with her sister, she could see that Jane was very unhappy. She still really loved Mr. Bingley.

The first week of Elizabeth's return was soon over. It was the last week of the regiment's stay in Meryton. Lydia received an invitation to go to Brighton from Mrs. Forster, the wife of the colonel of the regiment. Elizabeth secretly advised her father not to let Lydia go.

Mr. Bennet said, "Let her go. Colonel Forster is a sensible[5] man. He'll keep her out of trouble."

Elizabeth had to accept her father's decision.

Chapter 11

It was summer, and Elizabeth was looking forward to a tour of Derbyshire with her aunt and uncle, Mr. and Mrs. Gardiner.

However, it was impossible for her to see the word Derbyshire without thinking of Pemberley House and its owner, Mr. Darcy. "But surely," she thought, "I can visit his county without him knowing about it."

The day of their trip arrived. The Gardiners and Elizabeth traveled to Lambton, where Mrs. Gardiner used to live. Elizabeth found out from her aunt that Pemberley was five miles away, and Mrs. Gardiner wanted to visit the house again.

Elizabeth didn't want to go. There was always the possibility of meeting Mr. Darcy, and that would be awful! She decided to find out if he were at the house. So, when she went to bed that night, she asked the maid[6] at the inn[7].

"No, Madam. He's not there at the moment," said the maid.

Now Elizabeth felt curious about the house, so the next morning, she told her aunt that she would like to see Pemberley.

---

1 vain [ven] (a.) 自負的;虛榮的
2 unfortunate [ʌnˋfɔrtʃənɪt] (a.) 不幸的
3 rude [rud] (a.) 粗魯的;無禮的
4 regiment [ˋrɛdʒəmənt] (n.) 軍團
5 sensible [ˋsɛnsəbḷ] (a.) 明智的
6 maid [med] (n.) 侍女
7 inn [ɪn] (n.) 小旅館

Elizabeth nervously watched for the first appearance of Pemberley House. The park was very large, and they drove for some time through a beautiful wood. Finally, at the top of a hill, Elizabeth first saw Pemberley, on the opposite side of the valley. It was a large, handsome stone building with woods and hills behind it. Elizabeth loved it.

As they drove down the hill towards the house, all her fears of meeting its owner returned.

"What if the maid were wrong?" she thought.

They asked to see the house, and the housekeeper[1] agreed to show them round. All the rooms were beautiful, and the furniture was lovely.

"To think, I could have been mistress[2] of this house!" Elizabeth thought.

Her aunt called her to look at a picture.

"That," said the housekeeper, "is my master."

"I've heard a lot about your master," said Mrs. Gardiner, looking at the picture. "He's very handsome. But, Lizzy, you can tell us whether it's like him or not."

"Does the young lady know Mr. Darcy?" asked the housekeeper.

Elizabeth blushed, and said, "A little."

"And don't you think he's very handsome?"

"Yes, very handsome," said Elizabeth.

---

1 housekeeper [ˈhaʊsˌkipɚ] (n.) 女管家
2 mistress [ˈmɪstrɪs] (n.) 女主人

"Is your master often at Pemberley?" asked Mr. Gardiner.

"Not so often as I would like, sir," replied the housekeeper. "But we're expecting him here tomorrow."

"If your master married, you might see more of him," said Mr. Gardiner.

"Yes, sir; but I don't know who is good enough for him."

"That's a compliment," said Elizabeth.

"Everybody who knows him will agree with me," replied the housekeeper. Elizabeth listened with astonishment as the housekeeper added, "I've never heard an angry word from him, and I've known him ever since he was four years old."

Mr. Darcy was good-tempered[1]. Elizabeth wanted to hear more, and she was grateful to her uncle for saying, "You're lucky to have such a master."

"Yes, sir, I am. There isn't a better master in all the world."

Elizabeth stared at her. "Is this the same Mr. Darcy?" she wondered.

"Some people call him proud," the housekeeper continued, "but he isn't. People only think that because he doesn't chat away like other young men."

"This description[2] of him," whispered[3] her aunt as they walked, "isn't quite how *you* described him."

"No," replied Elizabeth.

---

1 good-tempered [ˈgʊdˈtɛmpɚd] (a.) 好脾氣的
2 description [dɪˈskrɪpʃən] (n.) 描繪;敘述
3 whisper [ˈhwɪspɚ] (v.) 低聲説

In the gallery of family **portraits**[1], Elizabeth walked in search of Mr. Darcy. At last she found him, with such a smile as she remembered seeing when he looked at her. She stood several minutes before the picture, deep in thought. As a brother, a **landlord**[2], a master, she considered how many people's happiness was in his hands! His eyes were on her, and she thought of his love for her with a deeper feeling of **gratitude**[3].

They returned downstairs, and said their goodbyes to the housekeeper before leaving the house.

Elizabeth

- How do you think Elizabeth feels now?
- What is Pemberley like?
- How is Mr. Darcy described?

As they walked across the garden towards the river, Elizabeth turned back to look at the house again; her uncle and aunt also stopped and looked, and as they were looking, Mr. Darcy suddenly appeared.

They were so close, and his appearance was so sudden, that it was impossible to avoid him.

(41)   Their eyes met, and they both blushed. He was so surprised, he couldn't move. He soon recovered, however, and spoke to her, if not calmly, at least politely. Elizabeth, didn't **dare**[4] lift her eyes again to his face, and she didn't know what answers she gave to his questions about her family. He was nervous too, and he kept repeating the same questions.

At length he couldn't think of anything more to say, and he suddenly **took leave**[5].

"He's such a good-looking man and so tall," Mrs. Gardiner said, but Elizabeth didn't hear her. She was lost in her own thoughts. "Oh, why did I come? And why did he come a day before he was expected?"

They were now on a beautiful path by the river, but Elizabeth saw nothing. Her thoughts were all fixed on Mr. Darcy. What did he think of her, and did he still love her?

They took the shorter walk around the park. Whilst walking, they were again surprised by the sight of Mr. Darcy approaching them. Elizabeth was determined to appear calm.

"What a lovely house you have," she said, and then she suddenly remembered that praise[6] of Pemberley might be misunderstood. She said no more.

Mr. Darcy started talking to Mr. Gardiner. The conversation turned to fishing; and she heard Mr. Darcy invite her uncle to fish there as often as he chose.

---

1 portrait [ˋportret] (n.) 肖像
2 landlord [ˋlænd͵lɔrd] (n.) 房東
3 gratitude [ˋgrætə͵tjud] (n.) 感恩
4 dare [dɛr] (v.) (aux.) 敢；竟敢
5 take leave 告辭
6 praise [prez] (n.) 稱讚

"Why is he being so polite? It can't be for *my* sake[1]. It's impossible that he still loves me," she thought.

After walking some time in this way, the two ladies in front, the two gentlemen behind, they changed places. Mr. Darcy and Elizabeth walked on together. After a short silence, Elizabeth was the first to speak.

"I was told you wouldn't be here," she said.

"I had some business with my steward[2] so I had to come early. My sister will join me here tomorrow," he continued, "and Mr. Bingley and his sisters are coming too."

Elizabeth answered with a nod.

"My sister would love to meet you. Will you come for tea tomorrow?"

Elizabeth was surprised. She immediately felt that the introduction was not Miss Darcy's wish but her brother's, and she was pleased. When they arrived back at the house, he invited them all in but they declined. Mr. Darcy helped the ladies into the carriage; and when it drove off, Elizabeth watched him walking slowly towards the house.

Elizabeth

- Why is Elizabeth now pleased?

The next day, Elizabeth and her aunt went to Pemberley to have tea with Georgiana Darcy and Miss Bingley. At the end of their visit, while Mr. Darcy was walking them to their carriage, Miss Bingley began to criticize Elizabeth. But Georgiana wouldn't join her. Her brother couldn't be wrong, and he **spoke very highly of**[3] Elizabeth. When Mr. Darcy returned to the living room, Miss Bingley repeated one of her **criticisms**[4].

"How very ill Elizabeth Bennet looks this morning, Mr. Darcy," she cried.

"I don't think so at all," said Mr. Darcy.

"I remember, when we first met her, how surprised we all were to hear her called a beauty; and you said, 'If *she's* a beauty, her mother's a **comedian**[5]!' But then you began to think she was pretty."

"Yes," replied Darcy, "but *that* was only when I first saw her. For months now, I've thought her to be one of the most beautiful women I know."

Mr. Darcy

- How does Mr. Darcy now feel?

---

1 for one's sake 看在某人的份上
2 steward ['stjuwəd] (n.) 管家；賬房
3 speak highly of . . . 對……評價很好
4 criticism ['krɪtə,sɪzəm] (n.) 批評；評論
5 comedian [kə'midɪən] (n.) 滑稽人物

Chapter 12

The next morning, Elizabeth received a letter from Jane. Her uncle and aunt had gone out for a walk and she was by herself.

"Dearest Lizzy, I've got bad news for you. Lydia has eloped with Mr. Wickham! Mr. Denny doesn't think Mr. Wickham intends[1] to marry Lydia. Colonel Forster has discovered they're in London. Please come home as soon as possible. Father's going to London with Colonel Forster to try and find her. I think he'll need my uncle's help. Please ask him to go to London.

"Oh, where's my uncle?" cried Elizabeth, jumping up from her chair. But as soon as she reached[2] the door, it was opened by a servant, and Mr. Darcy appeared.

"I'm sorry," she said, "but I must find Mr. Gardiner immediately."

"What's the matter?" he cried, looking at her pale face. "Let the servant go and find Mr. Gardiner. You aren't well enough to go yourself."

(45)   He was right. Elizabeth asked the servant to find Mr. and Mrs. Gardiner immediately.

"Shall I get you a glass of water?" Mr. Darcy asked kindly.

"No, thank you," she replied. Then she **burst into tears**[3]. "I've just had a letter from Jane, with awful news. My younger sister, Lydia has eloped with Mr. Wickham. She hasn't any money, nothing that can tempt him to marry her, she is lost forever."

"I'm very sorry," said Mr. Darcy, "upset, shocked. But is it certain, completely certain?"

"Oh, yes! They left Brighton together on Sunday night, and they're in London now."

"And what's been done to get her back?"

"My father's gone to London, and Jane's written to ask for my uncle's help. We'll leave, I hope, in half an hour. But nothing can be done. I know that."

Mr. Darcy was walking up and down the room in serious thought, on his brow a frown, his mood **gloomy**[4].

Elizabeth watched him, and immediately understood. "He can't love me now, not after this."

And in this moment of **despair**[5], she knew she loved him now, when all love must be **in vain**[6].

"I wish I could do something, anything that might make you feel better!" he said kindly.

---

1 intend [ɪnˈtɛnd] (v.) 想要;打算
2 reach [ritʃ] (v.) 到達
3 burst into tears 突然哭出來

4 gloomy [ˈglumɪ] (a.) 憂鬱的
5 despair [dɪˈspɛr] (n.) 絕望
6 in vain 徒然

(46) "Thank you," said Elizabeth. "Please apologize to Miss Darcy. Say that urgent business calls us home immediately. Hide the unhappy truth for as long as possible."

He promised not to tell anyone, and with one sad, parting look, left the room.

"I'll never see him again," thought Elizabeth. And she watched him go with regret[1].

Mr. and Mrs. Gardiner came back, and they left for Longbourn as soon as possible.

Mr. Wickham

- What are Mr. Wickham's faults?
- What do you think of his behavior?

1 regret [rɪˈgrɛt] (n.) 後悔
2 anxiety [æŋˈzaɪətɪ] (n.) 焦慮；掛念
3 arrange [əˈrendʒ] (v.) 安排
4 repay [rɪˈpe] (v.) 報答
　（動詞三態：repay; repaid; repaid）

Chapter 13

Every day at Longbourn was now a day of anxiety[2]. Mr. Bennet arrived home from London with no news of Lydia. Then, two days after his return, a letter came from Mr. Gardiner.

"They've found Lydia and Mr. Wickham," said Mr. Bennet. "Your uncle has arranged[3] for them to get married in London. I just need to give Lydia an income of one hundred pounds a year."

"That's wonderful news. Have you answered the letter?" Elizabeth asked.

"No, but I must answer it immediately. They must marry. But how much money has your uncle given?"

"Money!" cried Elizabeth. "What do you mean?"

"I mean, that no man would marry Lydia with only one hundred pounds a year."

"That's true," said Elizabeth. "My uncle must have given Wickham some money. The kind, generous man."

"Wickham's a fool if he takes her with less than ten thousand pounds," said Mr. Bennet.

"Ten thousand pounds! But how can we ever repay[4] him?" Mr. Bennet didn't answer.

48   Elizabeth's first thought was, "Why did I tell Mr. Darcy about Lydia's elopement? Now Lydia's getting married, nobody will know about the elopement."

She was miserable. "All I want is to hear from him," she thought. "But there's no chance of that. We'll probably never meet again. I proudly rejected his proposal. Now I would happily receive it again."

She began to understand that he was exactly the type of man she wanted to marry. "We were the perfect **match**[1]," she thought.

A few days later, Lydia arrived home with her new husband.

One morning, soon after their arrival, she said to Elizabeth, "Lizzy, I never told you about my wedding. Aren't you curious to hear about it?"

"Not really," replied Elizabeth; "I think there can't be too little said on the subject."

"Oh, you're so strange! But I must tell you about it. We were married at St. Clement's church. Mr. Darcy was there, and . . ."

"Mr. Darcy!" repeated Elizabeth, amazed.

"Oh, yes! He came with Wickham, you know. But, I'm not supposed to tell anyone. It's a secret!"

Elizabeth was curious now. Why had Mr. Darcy gone to Lydia's wedding? Quickly, she wrote a letter to her aunt, asking for an explanation.

---

1   match [mætʃ] (n.) 匹配者；相配

She soon received an answer.

"Mr. Darcy arranged the marriage. He paid all Mr. Wickham's debts[1], and he bought him a commission[2] in the army[3]. I thought you knew," wrote her aunt.

"Maybe he did it for me," Elizabeth's heart whispered.

But she didn't hope this for long. "He wouldn't do this for a woman who refused to marry him," she soon felt. "And he'd never make himself Wickham's brother-in-law[4]!"

Regrets

- What do Mr. Darcy's actions show about his character?
- What does Elizabeth regret?
- Have you ever regretted saying or doing something?

1 debt [dɛt] (n.) 債
2 commission [kə`mɪʃən] (n.) 軍官職位；委任
3 army [`ɑrmɪ] (n.) 軍隊；陸軍
4 brother-in-law [`brʌðərɪn‚lɔ] (n.) 連襟；姊夫；妹夫

Chapter 14

(50) The day of Mr. Wickham's and Lydia's **departure**[1] soon came. Mrs. Bennet was miserable but not for long. There was some exciting news. Mr. Bingley was coming to Netherfield again.

"As soon as Mr. Bingley comes," said Mrs. Bennet to her husband, "you'll visit him of course."

"Last year you promised, that if I went to see him, he'd marry one of my daughters—but he didn't. I'm not going to visit him again."

"Well, I'll ask him to dine here, anyway," said Mrs. Bennet.

"I'm beginning to wish he wasn't coming," said Jane to Elizabeth. "Everybody keeps talking about him."

On the third morning after Mr. Bingley's arrival, Mrs. Bennet saw him, from the window, riding towards the house.

Her daughters were called to come and see. Jane stayed at the table, but Elizabeth went to the window, she looked, she saw Mr. Darcy with him, and sat down again by Jane.

"There's a gentleman with him, Mamma," said Kitty. "It looks like that tall, proud man."

"Oh, no! It's Mr. Darcy!" said Mrs. Bennet.

Jane looked at Elizabeth with surprise. Both sisters were uncomfortable. Each **felt for**[2] the other.

To Elizabeth, Mr. Darcy was now the man who she loved almost as much as Jane loved Mr. Bingley. She was astonished that he was coming to Longbourn. A happy smile lit up her eyes.

"He must still like me," she thought. "But first, let me see how he behaves. Then I'll know how he feels."

She sat sewing[3], and trying very hard to stay calm.

Jane looked paler than usual. On the gentlemen's entrance[4], Jane blushed, but she greeted them calmly.

Elizabeth glanced once at Mr. Darcy. He looked very serious. Mr. Bingley looked both happy and embarrassed. He was greeted politely by Mrs. Bennet. Mr. Darcy, however, was greeted very coldly.

Elizabeth was hurt and embarrassed by her mother's coldness towards him. If only she knew that he had saved her dear Lydia from disgrace[5].

Mr. Darcy, after asking after Mr. and Mrs. Gardiner, said hardly anything. He wasn't sitting near Elizabeth; perhaps that was the reason for his silence.

When the gentlemen stood up to leave, Mrs. Bennet invited them to dine at Longbourn.

1 departure [dɪˈpɑrtʃɚ] (n.) 離開
2 feel for 有同感
3 sew [so] (v.) 做女紅
  （動詞三態：sew; sewed; sewn）
4 entrance [ˈɛntrəns] (n.) 進入
5 disgrace [dɪsˈgres] (n.) 丟臉；蒙羞

(52) Mr. Darcy's behavior had upset Elizabeth. "Why did he come? He didn't speak to me at all. He doesn't love me." Then she was angry with herself. "No man proposes twice to the same woman. They're too proud. I must stop thinking about him."

Prejudice

- Who shows prejudice and how?
- Have you ever been wrong about somebody's character?

1 easy-going [ˈizɪ,goɪŋ] (a.) 隨和的
2 cheat [tʃit] (v.) 欺騙
3 engagement [ɪnˈgedʒmənt] (n.) 訂婚

(53) A few days after his visit, Mr. Bingley called again, alone. Mr. Darcy had left that morning for London. Mr. Bingley stayed for dinner, and that evening he proposed to Jane.

"Oh, Lizzy, I'm the happiest girl in the world," said Jane. "Mr. Bingley has asked me to marry him."

Elizabeth's congratulations were given with great happiness.

After Mr. Bingley had left, Mr. Bennet turned to his daughter, and said, "Jane, congratulations! You'll be a very happy woman. Your characters are alike. You're both so **easy-going**[1], that no decisions will ever be made; so kind, that every servant will **cheat**[2] you; and so generous, that you will always spend more than your income."

"Spend more than their income! My dear Mr. Bennet," cried his wife, "that's not possible. Mr. Bingley has an income of four or five thousand a year."

Then speaking to her daughter, she said, "Oh! My dear Jane, I'm so happy! I was sure you couldn't be so beautiful for nothing!"

Mr. Bingley was a daily visitor at Longbourn, and the **engagement**[3] couldn't be a secret for long. Mrs. Bennet whispered it to Mrs. Phillips, and she whispered it to all her neighbors in Meryton.

"Oh, Lizzy! If only there were another such man for you!" said Jane.

(54) One morning, about a week after Mr. Bingley's engagement to Jane, a carriage drove up to the house. It was Mr. Darcy's aunt, Lady Catherine de Bourgh, and she was not happy. She wanted to speak to Elizabeth in private, so they went into the garden. "Miss Bennet, I've heard a terrible rumor[1]. Are you engaged[2] to my nephew?" she asked.

"I am not," replied Elizabeth, quietly.

"And will you promise me, never to become engaged to him?"

"I won't promise," said Elizabeth.

"I won't leave till you've promised," said Lady Catherine.

"And I'll *never* promise."

"I know all about your youngest sister's elopement," said Lady Catherine, angrily. "Is such a girl to be my nephew's sister? Is Mr. Wickham to be his brother? Is Pemberley to be so polluted[3]?"

"You can now have nothing further to say," said Elizabeth. "You've insulted me, and I must ask you to leave." Elizabeth stood up as she spoke.

Lady Catherine walked angrily to her carriage and left immediately.

The next morning, Elizabeth's father came out of his library with a letter in his hand. "Lizzy," he said, "I was just coming to find you. I've received a letter from Mr. Collins that has astonished me."

"What does *he* say?"

"Your daughter Elizabeth will soon be married to one of the most important and richest men in the country. Can you guess, Lizzy, who he means? *Mr. Darcy*! Mr. Darcy, who never looked at you in his life! It's very funny!"

Elizabeth didn't find it funny at all.

---

1 rumor [ˋrumɚ] (n.) 謠言;傳聞
2 engaged [ɪnˋgedʒd] (a.) 訂了婚的
3 polluted [pəˋlutɪd] (a.) 受污染的

(55) To Elizabeth's surprise, soon after Lady Catherine's visit, Mr. Darcy came to Longbourn.

Mr. Bingley, who wanted to be alone with Jane, suggested they all went out for a walk. Jane and Mr. Bingley walked ahead, leaving Elizabeth with Mr. Darcy.

Now was the moment for her to speak, "Mr. Darcy," she began, "I must thank you for your kindness to my sister, Lydia."

"You're not supposed to know about that," replied Mr. Darcy, surprised. "I thought I could trust Mrs. Gardiner."

"You mustn't blame my aunt. It was Lydia who told me," said Elizabeth. "Now, let me thank you, for all my family."

"Your *family* owe me nothing," he replied. "I did it for *you*, Elizabeth. If your feelings are still the same as last April, tell me at once. *I still love you*, but one word from you, will silence me on this subject forever."

"My feelings have changed," said Elizabeth awkwardly[1]. "I love you too."

Mr. Darcy had never felt so happy, and he expressed his feelings as strongly as a man madly in love[2] can do.

---

[1] awkwardly [ˈɔkwədlɪ] (adv.) 笨拙地
[2] madly in love 瘋狂愛戀

Love

- What made Elizabeth change her mind about Mr. Darcy?
- When did her feelings start to change?

(56) They walked on, not knowing in which direction. There was too much to be thought, and felt, and said.

"We must thank Lady Catherine for this. She told me you wouldn't promise to reject a proposal from me. It gave me hope," said Mr. Darcy, "I knew if you didn't want to marry me, you would tell Lady Catherine that."

Elizabeth laughed and replied, "You know me very well."

"Did my letter make you think better of me?" asked Mr. Darcy.

Elizabeth explained that after reading the letter, all her former prejudices had disappeared.

"You **taught me a lesson**[1]," said Mr. Darcy. "I was sure you would accept my proposal. You showed me I didn't have the character to make a woman **worthy**[2] of being loved, fall in love with me."

"Did you really think I'd accept you?"

"Yes. Can you believe my vanity? I thought you were hoping for it, expecting my proposal."

"You must have hated me after *that* evening."

"Hate you! I was angry at first, but that soon passed."

"And were you angry with me for coming to Pemberley?" Elizabeth asked.

"No, of course not. I was surprised. Of course, I fell in love with you again, about half an hour after seeing you," he replied.

After walking several miles, they looked at their watches and saw that it was time to go home.

"That night, Elizabeth told Jane everything.

"You're joking, Lizzy! You can't be engaged to Mr. Darcy!"

"I'm serious. He loves me, and we're engaged."

"Oh, Lizzy! It can't be true. I know how much you dislike him."

"*That's* all in the past."

Jane still looked amazed. "My dear Lizzy, are you sure you can be happy with him?"

"I've no doubt of that. We'll be the happiest couple in the world. But are you pleased, Jane?"

"Of course. Nothing could make Bingley or me happier. We thought it was impossible. But do you love him enough? Oh, Lizzy! Don't marry without love."

"Oh, yes! In fact, I love him better than I love Bingley."

1 teach sb a lesson 給了某人一個教訓
2 worthy [ˋwɝðɪ] (a.) 值得的

"My dearest sister, *be* serious. How long have you been in love with him?"

"I don't know. But I believe it began after I first saw the beautiful garden at Pemberley."

"Please, be serious," said Jane.

Elizabeth soon convinced Jane that she was in love with Mr. Darcy.

"Now I'm happy," said Jane, "for you'll be as happy as I am."

Marriage

- What does Jane say about marriage?
- Do you agree with her?

Chapter 17

59 "I don't believe it!" cried Mrs. Bennet, as she stood at a window the next morning, "Mr. Darcy is coming here again with our dear Bingley! Lizzy, you must go for a walk with him again."

Elizabeth almost laughed at such a convenient[1] suggestion.

As soon as they entered, Mr. Bingley shook hands with such warmth that there was no doubt that he knew about her engagement to Mr. Darcy. Aloud he said, "Mrs. Bennet, do you have any more lanes[2] in which Elizabeth might lose her way again?"

"I advise Mr. Darcy, Lizzy, and Kitty to walk to Oakham Mount," said Mrs. Bennet. "It's a nice long walk, and Mr. Darcy hasn't seen the view."

"I'm sure it will be too long a walk for Kitty," said Mr. Bingley. Kitty agreed.

Mr. Darcy expressed a great curiosity to see the view, and Elizabeth agreed to walk there with him. As she went upstairs to get ready, Mrs. Bennet followed her, saying, "I'm so sorry, Lizzy, but it's for Jane's sake. You only need to talk to him now and then[3]."

---

1 convenient [kən'vinjənt] (a.) 方便的
2 lane [len] (n.) 巷；小路
3 now and then 有時；偶而

Mrs. Bennet

- Does Mrs. Bennet understand Elizabeth's feelings?
- Does your mother understand your feelings?

During their walk, they decided to tell everybody that they wanted to get married.

"I'll ask your father for his consent[1] this evening," said Mr. Darcy.

"And I'll tell my mother," said Elizabeth.

In the evening, soon after Mr. Bennet went to the library, Mr. Darcy followed him.

Elizabeth felt very nervous. She was miserable till Mr. Darcy appeared again. Then, she saw his smile.

He came over to her and whispered, "Your father wants to see you in the library."

Elizabeth went straight away. Her father was walking up and down the room, looking worried.

"Lizzy," he said, "you've always hated Mr. Darcy. Why have you accepted his proposal?"

She told him that her feelings had changed.

"He's rich, of course, and you'll have more fine clothes and carriages than Jane. But will they make you happy?"

1 consent [kən'sɛnt] (n.) 同意

61 "Have you any other objection," asked Elizabeth, "than your belief that I don't like him?"

"None at all. We all know he's a proud, unpleasant man but if you like him..."

"I do like him," she replied, with tears in her eyes, "I love him. He isn't really proud. In fact, he's very kind. You don't know him properly. Please don't talk about him like that. It upsets me."

Mr. Bennet

- What consent does Mr. Darcy have to get from Mr. Bennet?
- Do you still have this custom in your country?

"Lizzy," said her father, "I've given him my consent. He's the kind of man, to whom I wouldn't dare refuse anything. But I know your character, Lizzy. You couldn't be happy, unless you respected your husband. I don't want to see you unhappily married."

Elizabeth reassured[1] him that she loved Mr. Darcy, and then she told him what Mr. Darcy had done for Lydia. He listened with astonishment.

1 reassure [ˌriəˈʃur] (v.) 使消除疑慮

"This has saved me a fortune. I'll offer to pay Darcy tomorrow. He'll tell me he did it for love, and that will be the end of the matter."

As Elizabeth left the room he said, "If any young men come for Mary or Kitty, send them in."

When her mother went up to her dressing room that night, Elizabeth followed her, and told her everything.

Mrs. Bennet sat very still. "Mr. Darcy! I can't believe it! Ten thousand a year! I'm so happy. Such a charming man, so handsome, so tall. Dear Lizzy, a house in town! Three daughters married! I'll go mad."

Elizabeth's mother followed her into her bedroom. "Lizzy," she cried, "what's Mr. Darcy's favorite dish? We'll have it for dinner tomorrow."

The next day passed much better than Elizabeth expected. Mrs. Bennet was in such awe[1] of her son-in-law that she agreed with everything he said.

Elizabeth was also pleased to see her father trying to get to know him better.

1 awe [ɔ] (n.) (v.) 敬畏；畏怯
2 spot [spɑt] (n.) 地點
3 impudence ['ɪmpjʊdəns] (n.) 粗魯無禮
4 liveliness ['laɪvlɪnəs] (n.) 充滿活力
5 feed up with . . . 受夠了……

Chapter 18

Elizabeth wanted to know how Mr. Darcy had fallen in love with her.

"When did you first realize you were in love?" she asked.

"I can't remember the hour, or the spot[2], or the look, or the words," he said. "It's too long ago. I was in the middle before I knew that I *had* begun."

"You didn't think I was beautiful, and I was always very rude to you. Tell me the truth. Did you admire me for my impudence[3]?"

"I admired you for the liveliness[4] of your mind," he said.

"I think, you were fed up with[5] women who were always flattering you. I interested you, because I wasn't like *them*. There! I've saved you the trouble of explaining it. Of course, you hadn't seen anything good in me. But nobody thinks of *that* when they fall in love."

"You were very good to Jane when she was ill at Netherfield."

"Dearest Jane! But tell me, why did you come to Netherfield again?"

"I told myself I came to see if Jane still loved Bingley. However, my real purpose was to see *you*."

64 "But why did you look as if you didn't care about me?" asked Elizabeth.

"Because you were serious and silent, and gave me no encouragement."

"But I was embarrassed," said Elizabeth.

"And so was I," said Mr. Darcy. "It was Lady Catherine who gave me hope."

"Lady Catherine has been very useful," said Elizabeth. "But do you think you'll ever have the courage to tell her that we're getting married?"

"I have to tell her, so, if you give me some paper, I'll write to her now."

"And if I didn't have a letter to write myself, I would sit and admire your handwriting, as another lady once did. But I have an aunt to write to, too."

Elizabeth wrote as follows:

I'm the happiest woman in the world. I'm even happier than Jane; she only smiles, but I laugh. Mr. Darcy sends you all the love in the world. And, my dear aunt, you are invited to Pemberley whenever you like.

Yours,
Elizabeth

Ⓐ Personal Response

📢 **1** Discuss each of the topics in pairs or in small groups.

[a] Did you enjoy reading the story? Why?/Why not?

[b] Jane Austen originally called this novel *First Impressions*. Why do you think she called it that? Discuss.

[c] What is your first impression of Mr. Darcy? How does your opinion of him change?

[d] What is your first impression of Mr. Wickham? How does your opinion of him change?

[e] What does the story show about life in Jane Austen's time? Would you like to have lived then? Why?/Why not? How has life changed today?

[f] The characters all have faults. Discuss their faults.
Jane doesn't show her feelings.
Mr. Bingley gives up too easily.
Mr. Darcy . . .

[g] Most of the characters show pride and most of the characters show prejudice. Look at each character and discuss.

❸ Comprehension

2 Tick (√) true (T) or false (F).

T F   (a)   Mr. Bennet didn't go and introduce himself to Mr. Bingley.

T F   (b)   Jane met Mr. Bingley at a dance.

T F   (c)   Everybody thought Mr. Darcy was more handsome than Mr. Bingley when they first saw him.

T F   (d)   Mr. Bingley didn't fall in love with Jane.

T F   (e)   Mr. Bingley's sisters didn't want him to marry Jane.

T F   (f)   After Mr. Bingley left Netherfield, Jane met him in London.

T F   (g)   Elizabeth learnt that Mr. Darcy stopped Mr. Bingley's relationship with Jane.

T F   (h)   Mr. Darcy had cruelly refused to pay for Mr. Wickham to study law.

T F   (i)   Mr. Wickham had tried to elope with Mr. Darcy's sister.

T F   (j)   Elizabeth blamed Mr. Darcy for Jane's unhappiness.

T F   (k)   Lydia refused to run away with Mr. Wickham.

T F   (l)   Mr. Darcy paid Mr. Wickham to marry Lydia.

T F   (m)   Mr. Bennet always thought that Elizabeth was in love with Mr. Darcy.

T F   (n)   Elizabeth happily accepted Mr. Darcy's second proposal.

3 Complete the sentences with the names of the characters.

Lydia Jane Miss Bingley

Mr. Darcy Georgiana Darcy Elizabeth

a _____ wanted to marry Mr. Darcy.

b _____ was stopped from eloping with Mr. Wickham.

c _____ eloped with Mr. Wickham.

d _____ was in love with Mr. Bingley.

e _____ didn't think Jane was in love with Mr. Bingley.

f _____ began to regret rejecting Mr. Darcy's marriage proposal.

4 Ask and answer these questions with a friend.

a Why did Elizabeth reject Mr. Darcy's first proposal of marriage?

b Why did Mr. Darcy separate Mr. Bingley and Jane?

c Why did Mr. Darcy dislike Mr. Wickham?

d What made Mr. Darcy hope that Elizabeth's feelings for him had changed?

e Why didn't Mr. Bennet want his daughter Elizabeth to marry Mr. Darcy?

f Why was Mrs. Bennet happy about Elizabeth's marriage?

C Characters

5 Write the adjectives next to the characters they are used to describe.

- easy-going
- intelligent
- silly
- proud
- jealous
- sweet
- polite
- fashionable
- giggly
- wild
- friendly
- unpleasant

Elizabeth Bennet

Jane Bennet

Lydia Bennet

Mr. Darcy

Mr. Bingley

Miss Bingley

6 Complete the sentences with the words below.
Then, circle the correct person.

> in awe   charming   in love
> in vain   good judge   teased

(a) Jane / Elizabeth **didn't look like a girl who was**

_____.

(b) Mr. Wickham / Mr. Darcy **could be very** _____.

(c) Mr. Bingley / Miss Bingley **loved** _____.

(d) Elizabeth / Mr. Bingley **thought she/he was a**
_____ **of character.**

(e) Mr. Lucas / Mr. Bennet **often** _____ **his wife.**

(f) **Mrs. Bennet was** _____ of Mr. Bennet / Mr. Darcy.

7 What is your opinion of the following characters?
Discuss in pairs or small groups.

Mr. Bennet

Mrs. Bennet

Elizabeth Bennet

Jane Bennet

Mr. Darcy

Mr. Bingley

Mr. Wickham

8 Mr. Darcy shows very different sides to his character in his public and private life. Look at the sentences about Mr. Darcy and write private (PR) or public (PU).

_____ (a) He was loving and caring to his servants and he was a good brother.

_____ (b) He was arrogant and didn't talk to people at the ball.

_____ (c) He showed kindness in saving Lydia's reputation.

_____ (d) He was very welcoming to Elizabeth's aunt and uncle at his family home.

_____ (e) He didn't dance with anyone besides Mr. Bingley's sisters at the first ball.

9 Choose one of the characters from the novel and write a description of him/her.

Name
....

Positive Qualities
....

Negative Qualities
....

Lesson Learnt
....

🅓 Plot and Theme

10 Put the events from the story in the correct order.

- Elizabeth and Mr. Darcy's story

_____ (a) Elizabeth blamed Mr. Darcy for Jane's unhappiness and Mr. Wickham's poverty. She rejected his first marriage proposal.

_____ (b) At the first ball, Mr. Darcy didn't want to ask Elizabeth to dance.

_____ (c) This time Elizabeth accepted his proposal. She realized that he was the perfect match for her.

_____ (d) Mr. Darcy fell in love with Elizabeth.

_____ (e) Elizabeth thought Mr. Darcy was proud and unpleasant, and she didn't like him.

_____ (f) Elizabeth began to fall in love with Mr. Darcy and she hoped that Mr. Darcy would propose to her again.

_____ (g) Mr. Darcy was still in love with Elizabeth and he proposed to her a second time.

_____ (h) Elizabeth learnt that Mr. Wickham was at fault and Mr. Darcy was in fact a good man.

11 One of the themes of the story is prejudice. Have you ever felt prejudice against a person or place? Were you proved wrong? Discuss in pairs or small groups.

12 Complete the sentences with the names of the characters. What do the quotes show about the characters' opinions on love and marriage? Discuss in pairs.

> Mr. Bennet
> Mrs. Bennet
> Elizabeth
> Jane
> Mr. Bingley
> Mr. Wickham
> Mr. Darcy

a) "I admired you for the liveliness of your mind," said _____.

b) "Mr. Darcy! I can't believe it! Ten thousand a year! I'm so happy," said _____.

c) "I know your character, Lizzy. You couldn't be happy, unless you respected your husband," said

_____.

d) "But do you love him enough? Oh, Lizzy! Don't marry without love," said _____.

e) She began to understand that he was exactly the type of man she wanted to marry. "We were the perfect match," thought _____.

f) "_____'s main interest in my sister was her fortune, which is thirty thousand pounds."

g) "I know _____ wasn't worried about Jane's lack of social position and wealth."

13 Read the quotations about pride and prejudice. Do you agree or disagree? Discuss with a partner and give reasons for your answers.

a) "Vanity is a weakness but pride—pride is always necessary," said Mr. Darcy.

b) "Mr. Darcy's pride is the cause of all Jane's unhappiness," said Elizabeth.

c) "I've been so blind, so prejudiced, so stupid," Elizabeth cried. "I've prided myself on being a good judge of character but I'm not!"

❤ Language

🗨 **14** Explain to a partner the meaning of the terms in the box.

flattered
consent
elope
rejected
insulted
the perfect match

15 Complete the sentences with words from Exercise **14**.

ⓐ Mr. Bennet gave his _____ to Mr. Darcy's marrying Elizabeth.

ⓑ Elizabeth _____ Mr. Darcy's first proposal.

ⓒ Mr. Darcy _____ Elizabeth's pride when he didn't ask her to dance.

ⓓ Mr. Wickham had planned to _____ with Mr. Darcy's sister.

ⓔ Elizabeth eventually realized Mr. Darcy was _____ for her.

ⓕ Jane was _____ by Mr. Bingley asking her to dance twice.

16 Match the everyday expressions from the story with their meanings.

_____ a take leave   ① not think it's somebody's fault

_____ b speak very highly of   ② be brave enough to

_____ c for (my) sake   ③ bored with

_____ d not blame somebody   ④ talk about something different

_____ e fed up with   ⑤ say goodbye and leave

_____ f have the courage to   ⑥ say good things about

_____ g change the subject   ⑦ to please/help (my)

17 Complete the sentences with the correct form of the verbs below.

a After Elizabeth's walk to Mr. Bingley's house, her dress _____ in mud.

b Elizabeth's refusal to dance with Mr. Darcy _____ his opinion of her.

c Before meeting Elizabeth, Mr. Darcy _____ so attracted to a woman.

d Mr. Wickham said that Mr. Darcy _____ his father's will.

e Mr. Darcy's first proposal _____ by Elizabeth.

f Mr. Darcy told Elizabeth that Mr. Bingley _____ Jane when he was in London because he _____ she was there.

> never be
> not know
> reject
> cover
> ignore
> not contact
> not affect

TEST

⭐ **1** How did the characters' feelings change?
Choose the correct answer 1, 2, 3 or 4.

_____ a At first, Elizabeth thought that Mr. Darcy had destroyed Mr. Wickham's life.
Then she learnt that . . .

① Mr. Wickham had become a successful lawyer.

② Mr. Wickham had wasted all the money Mr. Darcy had given him.

③ Mr. Wickham had become a vicar.

④ Mr. Wickham had stolen money from Mr. Darcy's father.

_____ b Elizabeth also learnt that . . .

① Georgiana Darcy had eloped with Mr. Wickham.

② Mr. Darcy had stopped his sister Georgiana Darcy from eloping with Mr. Wickham.

③ Mr. Wickham had been in love with Mr. Darcy's sister.

④ Mr. Wickham was married to Mr. Darcy's sister.

_____ c Elizabeth thought that Mr. Darcy was proud, selfish and bad-tempered. She learnt from the housekeeper that Mr. Darcy was . . .

① never angry and he wasn't proud either.

② a very good sportsman and liked fishing.

③ very clever and had won many awards.

④ a good farmer and loved animals.

_____ (d) Mr. Darcy didn't think that Jane loved Mr. Bingley. He thought that she . . .
① was about to elope with somebody else.
② wanted to marry Mr. Bingley for his money.
③ was in love with Mr. Wickham.
④ just enjoyed the attention.

2 Read the sentences below. Complete the second sentence so it means the same as the first. Use one word.

(a) After twenty-three years of marriage, his wife still didn't understand him.
After being _____ for twenty-three years, his wife still didn't understand him.

(b) Elizabeth didn't realize that she had an admirer.
Elizabeth didn't realize that somebody felt _____ for her.

(c) Miss Bingley was very critical of Elizabeth.
Miss Bingley often _____ Elizabeth.

(d) Mr. Bingley's sisters always dressed in the latest fashions.
Mr. Bingley's sisters were very _____.

(e) Elizabeth's younger sisters were often an embarrassment to her.
Elizabeth often felt _____ by the behavior of her younger sisters.

PROJECT WORK

Divide the class into groups. Each group chooses a topic from below to research and prepare a presentation for the rest of the class on the Interactive White Board or with a poster.

Love and marriage

Look at the different types of marriages in the novel: Bingley and Jane, Darcy and Elizabeth, Wickham and Lydia and Mr. and Mrs. Bennet. What are they based on? Physical attraction, financial security, love or money? Which in your eyes will be the most successful? Give reasons.

Fashion and lifestyle

Look at the different types of
clothes and hobbies in the book.
What do you think of them?
Discuss in small groups how
they are different to what you
wear and what you do.

作者簡介

珍·奧斯汀（Jane Austen）出生於 1775 年十二月。她的父親 George Austen 是英國國教的教區牧師，母親叫 Cassandra。她有七個兄弟姊妹，她在家排行倒數第二。奧斯汀一家人住在漢普郡（Hampshire）的史蒂文斯頓（Steventon），一家人都受過良好的教育，生活過得幸福和樂。珍跟與母親同名的姊姊感情很要好，我們對於珍·奧斯汀的瞭解，多半是從她跟姊姊的信件往返得知。

珍從十二歲起開始，便為家人撰寫故事和劇本，當作消遣。當她還是一位青少女時，便立志要當一名作家。

儘管珍·奧斯汀的小說描寫的主題都和婚姻有關，但她一生小姑獨處。珍在二十歲時，與一個名叫 Tom Lefroy 的年輕法律系學生戀愛，他們因為男方來漢普郡造訪親戚而結識。在這段短暫相處的期間，兩個人花了許多時間相處，不過男方的家人並不希望兩個人往來，因為珍並非出身自門第之家。他後來返回倫敦繼續念書，兩年後，娶了同學的妹妹為妻。

珍·奧斯汀在七年的時間內寫了六部偉大的小說，包括《理性與感性》（Sense and Sensibility, 1811）、《傲慢與偏見》（Pride and Prejudice, 1813）、《曼斯菲爾德莊園》（Mansfield Park, 1814）、《諾桑覺寺》（Northanger Abbey）和《勸導》（Persuasion）則是於 1817 年，在珍歿後出版。這些小說都以匿名方式出版，小說成名後，大家才知道作者的名字。 1816 年，珍患病，前往溫徹斯特（Winchester）看病，最後於 1817 年七月 18 日病逝，葬於溫徹斯特座堂。

本書簡介

《傲慢與偏見》（Pride and Prejudice）的初稿完成於 1796 年十月與 1797 年九月之間，書名最初是《第一印象》（First Impressions）。這部小說一直到 1813 年才出版，是珍·奧斯汀出版的第二部小說。當初在撰寫這部小說時，她只有二十一歲。這部小說仍是英國文學中最受歡迎的作品之一，銷售超過二千萬冊。《傲慢與偏見》當初以匿名方式出版，與《理性與感性》為同一個作者。

《傲慢與偏見》一書的背景，是發生於 18 世紀英國的愛情故事。內容為班奈特（Bennet）一家人和其五名待嫁女兒的故事。班奈特太太人生中最大的心願，就是見到五個女兒們出閣。她很高興見到住處附近新搬來一位英俊又有錢的單身漢，他和長女珍談了戀愛。然而，珍的妹妹伊莉莎白（Elizabeth），她聰明又機智，她和單身漢那位英俊而且更富有的友人達西先生（Mr. Darcy）初識時，她並不喜歡他，他們之間美妙的愛情，由此展開序幕。為了這段愛情，男方要克服自己的傲慢，女方要拋開自己的偏見。珍·奧斯汀在一封信中寫到她對伊莉莎白的看法：

「我得承認，她是文學作品中一個最令人讚賞的角色，我無法、或者說不知道該如何容忍那些無法欣賞她的人。」

第一章

P. 15

舉世公認，黃金單身漢一定想娶個妻子。

這樣的單身漢每搬到一處新地方，這個根深蒂固的真理就已經存在左鄰右舍的心裡，終有一天，他會娶進自己的某個女兒。

「親愛的班奈特先生，你聽說尼德菲莊園終於租出去的事嗎？」他的妻子一早就對他說。

「沒有。」班奈特先生回答。

「你難道不想知道是誰租的嗎？」他的妻子嚷道。

「我不想知道，但是你想要說給我聽，我不反對。」班奈特先生回答。

「是一個富有的年輕闊少爺租下的。」

「他叫什麼名字？」

「賓利先生。」

「他結婚了，還是單身？」

「當然是個單身漢！這個單身漢每年有四、五千鎊的收入，這難道不是我們家女兒的福氣嗎？」

「關女兒什麼事？」

「你怎麼這樣叫人討厭？你一定知道我在盤算他能夠娶我們的哪個女兒。」他的妻子回答。

P. 16

「這是他住到這裡來的原因嗎？」

「當然不是。不過他或許會看中我們的哪個女兒，這是你要去拜訪他的原因。」

「我看不出來有什麼理由要這麼做。」

「親愛的，你可是要替女兒們打算。」班奈特太太說。

「我不需要跑一趟，我只要給他捎封信，告訴他，他可以娶走我任何一個他看上的女兒。」

「班奈特先生，你真愛開我的玩笑。」他的妻子說。

「我希望你這輩子可以見到許多年輕的闊少爺搬到我們這個地方來。」

「你又不肯去拜訪他們，就算有二十個闊少爺搬來，又有什麼用。」

「等到有二十個闊少搬來，我一定會一個個去拜訪。」

班奈特先生生性幽默，儘管結縭二十三年，妻子仍摸不透他的心思。

她倒是一個容易被猜透的人，她這一生的大事，就是把她的女兒們都嫁出去。

事實上，班奈特先生是賓利先生的首批訪客，他承諾說，在兩個星期內會舉辦的一下場宴會上，他會把自己的夫人和女兒介紹給他認識。

班奈特先生和班奈特太太

- 這兩個人是如何的不同？
- 這兩個人的個性，你比較喜歡誰，為什麼？
- 你有認識結婚二十三年的人嗎？
- 他們彼此如何交談？

第二章

P.17

舞會在晚間開始舉行。賓利先生帶著兩個妹妹和另一位年輕男士一同出席。

賓利先生長得一表人才，親切和善，待人彬彬有禮。他的姊妹們是時髦、流行的年輕女子。他的友人達西先生立刻引起全場的注意，他身材高挑，相貌英俊，每年有一萬鎊的收入。女性賓客們都認為，他比賓利先生英俊得多。大半個晚上，大家都用著愛慕的眼神望著他，一直到最後，大家才發現他很驕傲。既然他擺出了一副討人厭的嘴臉，就算他家財萬

貫，還有個大房子，也挽救不了他。

賓利先生就友善親切多了，他每一場舞都要跳，舞會散得早，還令他一番氣惱，他提到要在尼德菲莊園舉辦一場舞會。他跟他的友人真是天壤之別！達西先生只跟賓利先生的姊妹們跳舞，不願別人介紹在場的其他女賓客給他認識。大家都斷定他是這世上最驕傲、最令人反感的人。

P.19

每個人都討厭他，尤其是班奈特太太，因為他羞辱了自己的女兒伊莉莎白。

伊莉莎白·班奈特有兩場舞沒有舞伴，當時她無意間聽見達西先生和賓利先生的談話。

「來吧，達西，你得跳支舞。」賓利先生說。

「你知道我討厭跳舞，除非是很熟的舞伴。你的姊妹都已經在跟別人跳舞，舞會上沒有其他好的女人可以跟我跳舞。」

「我可不這樣想，我還沒見過這麼多可愛的女子，其中幾個長得真是貌美。」賓利先生嚷道。

「跟你跳舞的，是舞會上唯一的漂亮女孩！」達西先生一面說，一面看著最年長的班奈特小姐。

「噢，珍的確是我見過最漂亮的女子！」賓利先生說：「但她還有一個妹妹，也很漂亮。」

「你是指哪一個？」達西先生一邊問，一邊轉過身，朝伊莉莎白望了一會兒。

接著，他回過身，冷冷地說著：「她長得還可以，但是沒有漂亮到足以打動我。我沒有心情去跟受到其他男人冷落的小姐跳舞。你最好回到珍的身邊，別把時間浪費在我身上。」

賓利先生聽了他的話，於是達西先生便走開了。

伊莉莎白一方面感到有些惱火，另一方面也因為個性活潑、調皮，便把這件事當成笑話那樣，描述給友人聽。

P. 20

班奈特一家都沉浸在舞會的歡樂中，班奈特太太很高興見到賓利先生跟珍跳了兩次舞。珍也和母親一樣高興，而伊莉莎白也為珍感到高興。年紀較輕的妹妹凱蒂、瑪麗和莉迪亞，她們在舞會上沒缺過舞伴，她們就只關心舞伴的事。一家人玩得盡興而歸。

當天晚上，珍和伊莉莎白獨處時，珍告訴妹妹，她很喜歡賓利先生。

「他溫柔敦厚、親切有禮、幽默風趣，是我見過最討人喜歡的人了！」

「而且長得還很帥，所以他真是太完美了。」伊莉莎白回答。

「他第二次邀請我跳舞時，我真是受寵若驚。」珍說。

「他覺得你比所有在場的姑娘都要漂亮不知多少倍。嗯，他的個性真的很好，我不反對你欣賞他。不過在你眼裡，每個人都是好人。」伊莉莎白說。

第三章

P. 21

盧卡斯家住在距離朗伯恩不遠的地方，班奈特一家人就住在這裡。他們家的長女夏洛蒂跟伊莉莎白很要好。

盧卡斯家和班奈特家，兩家的幾位小姐見了面，就愛談舞會的事。因此，舞會隔天上午，盧卡斯家的姊妹便前往班奈特家，跟他們家的姊妹交換意見，而達西先生成了主要的話題。

「隆格太太告訴我，達西先生坐在她身旁，半個鐘頭都沒跟她說話。」班奈特太太說。

「賓利小姐跟我說，他一向就話不多，除非是很熟的人。他對待知己是非常親切的。」珍說。

「我才不相信這番話，親愛的，大家都說他可驕傲了。」班奈特太太說。

「我倒不在乎他沒跟隆格太太說話，我介意的是他沒有跟伊莉莎白跳舞。」夏洛蒂說。

「麗茲，下回千萬別跟他跳舞。」她的母親說。

「我想我可以向你保證，我絕對不會跟他跳舞。」伊莉莎白說。

P. 22

「他的驕傲倒是不會使我生氣，自門第之家的權貴子弟表現驕傲，也是情有可原的。」夏洛蒂·盧卡斯說。

「這倒是真的。要是他沒有侮辱到我的驕傲，我也可以輕易原諒他的驕傲。」伊莉莎白回答。

「驕傲是常人的通病。我們很少不會因為什麼事而感到驕傲。」瑪麗說。

驕傲

• 驕傲是好事，還是壞事？
• 有任何事令你感到驕傲嗎？

只要見到珍和賓利先生在一起，任誰看得出他的確是愛她的，伊莉莎白也看得出來，珍也很愛慕賓利先生。不過，她很確定目前並沒有任何人看出這一點。而她把這件事告訴了好友夏洛蒂。

「要是一個女人對於心愛的男人不表露自己的心意，那她就可能沒機會博得對方的歡心。賓利先生絕對很欣賞你的姊姊，你姊姊應該給他一些鼓勵。」夏洛蒂說。

「夏洛蒂說得沒錯，賓利先生可能不知道珍也很愛慕他。」伊莉莎白心想。

P. 23

現在，伊莉莎白的思緒都在珍的身上，她沒有想過自己也會有愛慕者。達西先生一開始並不覺得伊莉莎白長得很漂亮。不過，他後來開始發現她很聰慧。他注意到她有一雙烏黑發亮的眼睛，開始欣賞她的風趣。但是對她來說，他不過是個認為她不夠漂亮、不夠資格與他跳舞的男人。

達西先生希望對她有多一點的瞭解，所以開始偷聽她跟別人的談話。伊莉莎白注意到這一點，是有一天晚上在威廉·盧卡斯爵士家的宴會上。

「為什麼達西先生要偷聽我跟佛斯特上校的談話？」伊莉莎白問夏洛蒂。

「這個問題只有達西先生自己能夠回答。」夏洛蒂說。

「要是他再這樣，我一定會告訴他我發現了他的行徑。」

不久後，達西先生走上前來。

伊莉莎白轉過身，對他說：「達西先生，你難道不認為我剛才跟佛斯特上校提到在梅利頓舉辦一場宴會的事，說得很得體？」

「是很得體，不過女人家老愛談論這一類的話題。」他回答。

「你對我們女人真是刻薄。」伊莉莎白說。

眼見一場爭執就要展開，夏洛蒂立刻轉移話題。「我要彈奏一首鋼琴曲目，麗茲。」

P. 24

莉迪亞和凱蒂要她彈奏一些適合跳舞的曲目，在場的人開始跳起舞來。

達西先生站在一旁觀看，威廉‧盧卡斯爵士站在他的身邊。這時，伊莉莎白走向他們。

「達西先生，容我向你介紹班奈特小姐。她是非常優秀的舞伴。」威廉爵士說。

「我一點也不想要跳舞。」伊莉莎白說。

「可是你的舞跳得很好，伊莉莎白小姐。雖然達西先生不喜歡跳舞，不過他沒有理由不賞臉跟你共舞。」威廉爵士說。

伊莉莎白揚起她的眉毛，「是這樣嗎？」伊莉莎白說完便轉身走開。

在達西先生看來，她拒絕跳舞，這並沒有傷害到他自己，他正開心地想著她。這時。賓利小姐走過來說：「我能猜到你心裡在想什麼？」

「你恐怕猜想不到吧。」他回答。

「你一定在想，今天晚上真是無聊。我同意你的看法。」

「你完全猜錯了，我正在想著其中一位小姐的一雙烏黑眼睛。」

「是哪一位小姐呢？」賓利小姐問。

「伊莉莎白‧班奈特小姐。」達西先生回答。

第四章

P. 25

隔天，尼德菲莊園捎來一封信給班奈特小姐。

「珍，是誰寄來的信？」她的母親問。

「是賓利小姐，她邀請我去吃晚餐。她的哥哥和達西先生會外出用餐。」珍說。

「外出用餐，真是不湊巧。」班奈特太太說。

「我可以乘坐馬車去嗎？」珍問。

「不，親愛的，你最好騎馬去，因為看樣子要下雨了。到時候，你就可以留在賓利家過夜。」她的母親說。

珍騎馬前往赴約，這時開始下起傾盆大雨。珍的妹妹們很擔心她，但是她的母親卻很開心。大雨持續下了一整晚，珍果然留在對方家。

「多虧我想出來的點子！」班奈特太太說。

不過，隔天上午伊莉莎白收到了一封信。

「珍得了重感冒，我要立刻前往賓利家。」伊莉莎白嚷道。

「親愛的，如果你的女兒因此送命，你應該會感到安慰，這都是因為賓利先生的緣故。」班奈特先生說。

「人才不會因為傷風就送命。」班奈特太太說。

然而由於伊莉莎白實在太過擔心珍的病情，所以她親自走了一趟尼德菲莊園。

P. 26

當她抵達時，她被引進餐廳，受到賓利先生和他兩個妹妹的熱情款待。

因為珍病得很重，所以伊莉莎白便立刻上樓去探望她。

三點鐘時，伊莉莎白覺得應該要告辭了，不過珍捨不得讓她走。

賓利小姐邀請她在尼德菲莊園小住幾天，派遣僕人前往朗伯恩通知班奈特家這件事，並要家裡給她帶幾件衣服過來。

六點半時，伊莉莎白下樓吃晚餐。珍的病況仍未好轉，賓利先生很擔心。

用過晚餐之後，伊莉莎白再次前去陪伴珍，賓利小姐一等她離開餐廳，便開始批評她。

「她不懂禮節，不善交談，不懂得打扮，也沒有姿色。」

賓利小姐的姊姊，赫斯特太太也有同感，她補充說：「她今天早上那副模樣，真叫人難忘，簡直像個瘋子。」

「的確，露易莎，她的頭髮真是一團亂。」

「是啊，她的襯裙也沾滿了泥巴。」

「我認為伊莉莎白‧班奈特小姐今天早上看起來很好，我沒注意到她的裙襬有多髒。」賓利先生說。

「你一定注意到了，達西先生，我很確定。」賓利小姐說：「恐怕她這趟徒步之行，會影響到你對她那雙美麗眼睛的愛慕吧。」

「一點都沒有，這趟路讓她那雙眼睛更加明亮了。」他回答。

P. 28

屋內的人緘默了一會兒。

「珍・班奈特小姐真是一個很甜美的女孩，我由衷地希望她能夠嫁一個好人家。」赫斯特太太說：「只可惜遇到那樣的父母，這門親事應該沒指望了。」

「你不是說過她們的姨丈在梅利頓當律師。」賓利小姐說。

「他們還有另外一個舅舅住在倫敦的齊普賽街附近。」

「真妙。」她的妹妹說了這麼一句，然後姊妹倆相視大笑。

「即使她們的舅舅多到塞滿齊普賽街，也絲毫不會減損她們的魅力。」賓利先生嚷道。

「但是卻會減少她們嫁給有錢人家的機會。」達西先生回答。

賓利先生沒有接話，但是他的姊妹們都表示贊同。

批評

- 賓利小姐和赫斯特太太批評伊莉莎白什麼？
- 這一點顯示出她們擁有什麼樣的性格？

第五章

P. 29

隔天晚上，伊莉莎白加入客廳的一場聚會。達西先生正在寫信，賓利小姐坐在他身邊看他寫。伊莉莎白聆聽他們之間的對話，感到很有意思。

「你的手寫字跡真工整。」賓利小姐說。

達西先生沒有答腔。

「達西小姐收到這樣一封信，一定會很高興！」賓利小姐說。

他沒有回答。

「請轉告令妹，我很想跟她見面。」

「我已經轉告過她了。」

「你總是寫這樣一封文情並茂的長信給她嗎，達西先生？」

「我的信一向寫得很長，不過是不是每一封都文情並茂，我就不知道了。」他把信寫完之後，把筆放下。

接著，他請求賓利小姐彈奏幾首樂曲，賓利小姐飛快走到鋼琴邊坐下。

賓利小姐在彈奏鋼琴時，伊莉莎白忍不住留意到，達西先生的眼神總是望著自己。這真是不尋常，原因絕對不可能是因為他喜歡她。最後她只得這樣想，他一定是看到她哪一點不順眼。伊莉莎白也並不因此感到沮喪，因為她根本就不喜歡他。

P. 31

不過，從來沒有一個女人像伊莉莎白這樣令達西著迷。他打心裡認為，要是她出身好人家，那他就難以避免陷入愛情的危險。

賓利小姐感到十分忌妒，她希望珍可以快點復原，好讓伊莉莎白快點回家。

115

吃過晚餐以後，珍便坐到客廳去。賓利先生很高興見到她，他在珍的身邊坐下來，幾乎沒有跟其他人交談。伊莉莎白很高興地望著他們兩人。

喝過茶後，達西先生拿起一本書來。賓利小姐也跟著拿起一本書，卻沒有興趣閱讀手上的書。賓利小姐之所以挑選這本書，原因不過是這本書是達西先生那本書的第二卷。

她環顧客廳四周，想要找其他的消遣，這時突然聽見她的哥哥正在跟珍討論要開一場舞會的事。她轉過身去，望著他問：「你當真要在尼德菲舉辦舞會嗎？我覺得你應該先徵求在場友人的意見，不是每個人都喜歡舞會的。」

「如果你指的是達西先生，他可以在舞會開始前就上床睡覺。我們一定會舉辦一場舞會，就這麼決定。」她

的哥哥嚷道。

賓利小姐沒有回答，沒多久，她站起身來，在房間裡來回踱步。達西先生則是繼續念著他手中的書。賓利小姐決定做最後的努力，博得他的注意。

「伊莉莎白，你來跟我一道在屋內走一走。」她說。

P.32

伊莉莎白感到詫異，不過欣然同意她的邀請。

這回，賓利小姐的計謀成功了。達西先生果然抬起頭來，闔上他的書。

賓利小姐邀請他加入她們的行列，可惜遭到他的婉謝。

「我可以猜想到你們倆一塊在屋內走動，無非出於兩個動機。」

「他這話是什麼意思？」賓利小姐問：「你知道嗎，伊莉莎白？」

「我不知道，不過要讓他失望的最好辦法，就是不要叫他解釋。」伊莉莎白說。

賓利小姐說什麼也不願意讓達西先生失望，於是要求他解釋所謂的兩個動機。

「你們如果不是要說什麼悄悄話，就是想要展現你們的體態。如果是出於第一個原因，我願意加入你們的行列；如果是第二個原因，那麼我坐在火爐邊欣賞你們就行了。」達西先生說。

「唉呀，你説這話，真嚇壞人了！該怎麼處罰他？」賓利小姐嚷道。

「如果你真想要處罰他，只要譏笑他一番不就得了。」伊莉莎白説。

「但我們可不能嘲笑達西先生這樣的人。」

「真是可惜，我很喜歡開開玩笑。」伊莉莎白嚷道。

「就算是最聰明的人，也是會被愛取笑人的人所取笑。」達西先生説。

P. 33

「那是當然的。但我是絕對不會去取笑聰明或是善良的人，我只會譏笑那些擁有虛榮和傲慢這樣缺點的人。」伊莉莎白回答。

「虛榮的確是缺點，不過傲慢有其必要。」達西先生説。

伊莉莎白轉過頭去，免得讓人發現她在竊笑。

「我想你考問完達西先生了吧，請問結論是什麼？」賓利小姐説。

「達西先生沒有缺點，他自己也這麼説。」

「我有很多缺點，別人要是得罪了我，我不會輕易原諒對方或是忘記這件事。我對某個人沒有好感，就永遠不會有好感。」達西先生説。

「這倒是很大的缺點！」伊莉莎白也表示同意，「不過你對自己的缺點已經很嚴格挑剔了，我不能夠再譏笑你了。」

「我們來聽點音樂吧。」賓利小姐嚷道，厭倦這場談話沒她説話的份。

鋼琴打開了，達西先生感到鬆了一口氣。他開始感覺到，對伊莉莎白投注太多的注意力，是一件很危險的事。她對他的吸引力，超過他能夠承受的程度。

隔天，珍和伊莉莎白便離開尼德菲莊園。

第六章

P. 34

這天早上，用過早餐後，班奈特家的姊妹們決定步行到梅利頓，去拜訪她們的姨丈。

來到梅利頓之後，她們的注意力全都放在跟丹尼先生一塊行走的年輕英俊軍官身上。丹尼先生將他的友人韋克翰先生介紹給她們認識。大夥站在原地談得很投機，這時，達西先生和賓利先生正騎著馬從街上過來。

兩位紳士見到人群當中的幾位小姐，上前寒暄一番。

「我正打算前往朗伯恩拜訪你。」賓利先生對珍説。

達西先生的目光自然地望著伊莉莎白時，當他正要將目光移開時，突然看到了韋克翰先生。伊莉莎白看見兩個人臉上同時出現大驚失色的表情，一個變得蒼白，另一個漲紅了臉。這

117

是什麼意思呢？

過了一會兒，賓利先生便跟大夥告別，跟友人騎著馬離開。

丹尼先生和韋克翰先生陪著幾位年輕的小姐，一塊走到她們的姨丈家門口，才告辭離開。

P. 36

當她們步行返家時，伊莉莎白和珍談論起達西先生和韋克翰先生之間的尷尬場面。

隔天晚上，五個姊妹在姨丈家吃飯時，女孩們很高興聽見韋克翰先生和其他駐紮的軍官也要前來用餐。參加這次宴會的人物都是軍官之中的佼佼者。

「不過，韋克翰先生在相貌上遠超過其他人。」伊莉莎白心想。

韋克翰先生是當天的宴會中最出風頭的男子，幾乎在場的每個女人都在盯著他瞧，當韋克翰先生最後在她身邊坐下時，伊莉莎白成為當天宴會上最令人稱羨的女人。

當大夥開始玩牌時，韋克翰先生和伊莉莎白開始交談。伊莉莎白很想知道他過去跟達西先生之間的關係。出人意料的是，韋克翰先生主動談起這件事。

「達西先生待在尼德菲莊園多久了？」他問。

「大概有一個月了，你跟他很熟嗎？」伊莉莎白說。

「是的。我的父親替他的父親處理財產方面的事，所以我們從小在一起長大。」韋克翰先生回答。

伊莉莎白一臉詫異。

「你可能很詫異，班奈特小姐，你昨天見過我們見面時的場面。你跟達西先生很熟嗎？」

「跟他也不用太熟，我覺得他很不討人喜歡，他一點都不喜歡這裡。」伊莉莎白說。

P. 38

「老達西先生是一位很和善親切的人，他也很提拔我。他在遺囑上說，一旦郡裡的牧師肥缺空出來，就要給我，達西卻把這個職位給了其他人。」韋克翰先生說。

「真是太過分了！他怎麼能夠不遵

118

照遺囑去做？」伊莉莎白嚷道。

「那不是正式的遺囑，加上他很討厭我。」韋克翰先生說。

「但他為什麼討厭你？」

「他忌妒他的父親對我的愛護。」

「真是豈有此理！」伊莉莎白說。

他們倆一直談到吃晚餐的時候，在場其他女子才有機會分享韋克翰先生的殷勤。每個人都喜歡他。

韋克翰

- 韋克翰先生對伊莉莎白說了什麼？
- 伊莉莎白怎麼想？
- 你認為韋克翰先生是什麼樣的人？為什麼？

第七章

P. 39

尼德菲莊園舉辦宴會這一天終於到來。珍十分期待能和賓利先生共度這個夜晚，伊莉莎白則期待與韋克翰先生一起共舞。

伊莉莎白一抵達尼德菲莊園，遍尋不到韋克翰先生，於是便向丹尼先生打聽。

「韋克翰先生有事上倫敦了。在我看來，他是為了要迴避達西先生。」丹尼先生告訴伊莉莎白。

伊莉莎白因此斷定達西先生是造成韋克翰先生缺席的原因。因此當達西上前向她問好時，她簡直無法對他好聲好氣，連帶地對賓利先生的禮貌也不夠周到。不過，伊莉莎白的不悅並未持續太久。

跟夏洛蒂·盧卡斯談過之後，她感覺好過了些。當達西先生上前邀請她跳舞時，她跟夏洛蒂正有說有笑。她對自己竟接受他的邀舞，感到很吃驚。

當伊莉莎白下了舞池後，她仍對於跟達西先生面對面跳舞感到吃驚。他們站了一會兒，一句話也沒說。於是她就聊起了跳舞的話題，達西回答了之後，接著又是一陣沉默。

P. 41

停頓一會兒之後，她說：「現在輪到你說句話，達西先生。我談過了跳舞的話題，你可以談談舞池的大小或是舞伴的數目。」

他笑了笑問：「你跟你的姊妹們經常步行去梅利頓？」

「是啊，你那天看見我們時，我們正巧遇見韋克翰先生。」她回答。

達西先生漲紅了臉，皺起眉頭。

「韋克翰先生交友總是得心應手。至於能不能維持友誼，那就說不準了。」他說。

「我聽說，他很不幸地失去了你的友誼。」伊莉莎白回答。

達西先生沒應聲。這時,威廉·盧卡斯爵士走近他們身邊,說道:「你跟這位美麗的舞伴真相配,達西先生。我希望能夠有眼福常見到你們一塊跳舞,特別是一椿好姻緣即將發生(他朝珍和賓利先生望了一眼)。」

威廉爵士的這番話,令達西先生一臉憂愁。之後,他看著賓利先生和珍。他轉過身,對伊莉莎白說:「抱歉,我忘了我們剛剛談了些什麼。」

「我們根本沒談什麼,我們已經談了兩三個話題,總是話不投機。我現在實在不知道要談什麼。」

「我們不妨來談談書。」達西笑道。

「談書!噢,不,我相信我們涉獵的書不同,體會也不一樣。」

P. 42

「很遺憾你這麼想。要真是那樣,我們可以把不同的意見拿來相比。」

「不,我無法在跳舞時談論書本。」伊莉莎白沉默了一會說:「達西先生,我記得你說過,你幾乎不原諒別人。希望這一點並不是經常發生。」

「不常發生。」他說。

「你難道從沒受到偏見的蒙蔽嗎?」

「我希望不會。」

「對於容易對他人產生成見的人來說,在一開始做出評論時,應該格外慎重。」伊莉莎白說。

「這話的用意何在?」達西先生問。

「不過是想要對你的個性有所瞭解。」她說。

「那麼你究竟瞭解了沒?」

她搖搖頭,「我聽說很多對你不同的看法,叫我不知如何是好。」

「真令人難以置信,我希望你現在還不要對我的個性下定論,因為這麼做可能有失公允。」他回答。

「可是說不定以後就沒有機會了。」伊莉莎白回答。

「我不想要破壞你的興致。」他冷冷地說。

兩人跳完舞之後,默默離開,彼此很不快樂。然而,達西先生對伊莉莎白有強烈的好感,所以一下子就原諒她了,於是把一肚子怒氣轉向韋克翰先生。

P. 43

伊莉莎白將注意力放在開心的事物——她的姊姊和賓利先生身上。她此時想像著珍的婚姻過得幸福美滿，住在這棟宅邸裡。她的母親也正想著同樣的事。

當大家坐下來吃東西的時候，伊莉莎白無意間聽見她的母親對盧卡斯夫人信口說著珍將會跟賓利先生結婚之類的話。

伊莉莎白看見這段談話被達西先生聽見，他看去一臉不以為然的模樣。伊莉莎白感到一臉困窘。事實上，伊莉莎白覺得，她的家人像是說好了今天到這裡來出盡洋相似的。妹妹瑪麗五音不全，卻堅持要唱歌，凱蒂和莉迪亞老是在發傻的咯咯笑著。

伊莉莎白只想要回家去，但是她的母親卻堅持班奈特家要最後才離開舞會。等其他人都離開之後，他們家的馬車十五分鐘後才抵達。

後來，他們終於起身告辭，班奈特太太邀請賓利先生哪天到朗伯恩一起共餐。

「謝謝你，我會盡快赴約，不過明天我得動身前往倫敦。」他說。

第八章

P. 44

隔天，珍收到一封信。珍讀著信時，伊莉莎白看著姊姊臉色大變。「這封信是卡洛琳・賓利寫來，他們一家人離開尼德菲莊園，去了倫敦。」她說。

「別擔心，珍，賓利先生不會在倫敦待太久。」

「但你還不知道全部的真相。聽聽這裡。達西先生想要去見他的妹妹，我們也很想見見她。喬琪亞安娜・達西是一個容貌無人能比的年輕小姐。露易莎跟我都希望她很快可以成為我們的嫂嫂，我哥哥也很愛慕她。」珍說。

「你怎麼看這件事，麗茲？」珍問道：「卡洛琳不希望我成為他們的嫂嫂，這一點難道還不夠清楚嗎？而且她十分確定他的哥哥已經對我失去興趣。」

「這一點我不同意。賓利小姐明知道她的哥哥愛的是你，但是她希望她的哥哥能夠娶喬琪亞安娜・達西。」伊莉莎白說。

珍搖搖頭。

「你得相信我，珍。每個人都看得出來他愛上你。如果賓利小姐看出達西先生對她的愛有這樣一半的話，她就要準備出嫁了。」

P. 46

美滿的婚姻

• 賓利小姐為什麼要寫這封信給珍？
• 她為什麼希望她的哥哥娶達西小姐？

121

「但是麗茲，我要嫁的人，他的姊妹和朋友都希望他的結婚對象是別人，這樣的婚姻我還會幸福嗎？」

「如果擔心得罪他的姊妹所招致的痛苦，會比起成為一個幸福的妻子還要大的話，那麼你就不該嫁給他。」伊莉莎白說。

「但你也知道我會毫不猶豫地嫁給他的。」珍笑著說。

「我知道。既然這樣，我也就不必替你感到遺憾。」

同一星期，她們的舅媽卡帝納太太，邀請珍到她位於倫敦的寓所小住，珍一想到有機會在那裡見到賓利先生，不免感到一陣興奮。不過，一個月過去了，珍與賓利先生根本沒有見上一面。與他結婚的一切念頭成了空想，珍過得很不快樂。

第九章

P. 47

三月時，伊莉莎白受邀與友人夏洛蒂和她的新婚丈夫柯林斯先生同住，他們的牧師住宅是屬於凱薩琳·德·包爾夫人所有。復活節到了，凱薩琳夫人的外甥達西先生要前來拜訪他的姨媽，他將是凱薩琳夫人羅辛茲晚宴中新加入的座上賓。

「見到賓利小姐嫁給達西先生的機會變得渺茫，一定很有意思。凱薩琳夫人告訴我，他註定要娶她的女兒。」伊莉莎白心想。

達西先生的表哥費茲威廉上校也跟他一道前往羅辛茲。令大家感到驚訝的是，兩位賓客也將去牧師家拜訪。

「這次貴客臨門，都是託你的福，否則達西先生絕對不會這麼快就來拜訪我。」夏洛蒂說。

經過這次的拜訪之後，伊莉莎白多次在晚宴和在羅辛茲莊園漫步時，見到達西先生和他的表哥。一天，當她在莊園間穿梭時，碰巧遇上費茲威廉上校，於是便一塊步行到牧師住宅。

「你要在星期六離開羅辛茲嗎？」伊莉莎白問。

「沒錯，只要達西不要再把時間往後延。」費茲威廉上校回答。

P. 48

在回牧師住宅的一路上，費茲威廉

上校和伊莉莎白聊著天。閒談之間，伊莉莎白才知道，達西先生阻止友人免於一場不幸福的婚姻。

「那位小姐的家庭，受到了男方家人的強烈反對。」費茲威廉上校告訴她。伊莉莎白很確定他口中的這位友人是賓利先生，她心想，「我知道，達西先生阻止賓利先生跟珍見面。他的傲慢是造成是造成珍不快樂的原因。」她感到很氣憤。

返回牧師住宅後，她大哭了一場，還引發頭痛。當天晚上，她不想要見到達西先生，因此決定在羅辛茲的晚宴中缺席。

晚上時，伊莉莎白把珍最近寄給她的信又讀了一遍。至少，達西先生很快就要離開羅辛茲，不到兩個星期之後，她就可以再見到珍。

這時，門鈴突然響起，達西先生走進屋內。伊莉莎白感到十分詫異。達西先生向她問候，她基於禮貌，態度冷淡地回答他。

他坐下來一會後，又起身在房裡踱步。沉默了一會之後，才開口說：「我努力試著把自己的感覺隱藏起來，但是我再也藏不住了。我愛你。」

伊莉莎白吃驚地說不出話。她瞪大了眼睛，漲紅了臉，沉默不語。

P. 49

她的沉默讓他鼓起勇氣繼續往下說，他把自己對她的所有感覺都說了

出來。不幸的是，他不只表達他的愛意，他也提到她的家庭貧困、社會階級很低的事。

「儘管如此，我發現自己無法停止愛你。你願意嫁給我嗎？」他說。

「他十分確定我會接受他的求婚。」伊莉莎白心想。一想到這個，不禁令她感到惱怒，於是她說：「不，我不能夠嫁給你。」

求婚

- 你認為伊莉莎白會接受或是拒絕？
- 如果某個人以這樣的方式跟你求婚，你會怎麼做？

達西先生一臉吃驚。他的臉色發白，她能夠從他的眼裡見到他很受傷。他一時語塞，說不出話來。四周靜得可怕。

最後，他開口說：「我想知道你為何拒絕我。」

「你對我說過，你不想要愛我。此外，我不能夠嫁給摧毀我姊姊幸福的男人。」伊莉莎白回答說。

P. 50

聽見伊莉莎白這麼說，達西先生臉色發青。

「你對拆散珍和賓利先生的事，要加以否認嗎？」她問。

「我不否認，我對待他，比對待我

自己仁慈。」他語氣平靜說。

「這並不是讓我討厭你的唯一理由。」伊莉莎白繼續往下說:「你還毀了韋克翰先生的一生。」

「你對那位先生倒是挺感興趣的。」達西先生不怎麼高興地說。

「任何知道他的不幸遭遇的人,都會對他感興趣。」伊莉莎白回答。

「他的不幸遭遇?的確,他的遭遇的確很不幸。」達西先生語帶嘲諷說。

「這都要怪你使他成為一個不幸的人。」伊莉莎白喊道。

達西先生喊道:「這就是你對我的看法嗎?我知道我傷害了你的自尊,但是我對於向你告白的話,絲毫不感到羞愧。難道你期望我對於你的家庭感到開心嗎?」

伊莉莎白這時很火大,但仍勉強自己冷靜地說道:「沒有任何事可以讓我接受你的求婚。」

達西先生一臉不可置信望著她,感到十分困窘。

P. 51

她繼續往下說:「你傲慢又自私,從不顧及他人的感受。認識你一個月後,我就覺得,就算全世界的男人只剩下你一個,我也不會嫁給你。」

「你說夠了,小姐。我很清楚你的感受。原諒我佔據你這麼多的時間,祝你健康安好。」說完這番話之後,他便離開了。

之後,伊莉莎白坐了下來,哭了半個鐘頭。達西先生竟然跟她求婚!這幾個月來,他已經愛上了她!愛意已經深刻到要與她共結連理,儘管另一方面對她的家庭不敢苟同。真是令人不可思議!但是他的傲慢真是令人不敢恭維。珍因為他無法獲得幸福,韋克翰先生受到了他的殘酷對待。不!她絕對不可能嫁給他。

達西先生

- 你覺得達西先生的感受如何?
- 你認為伊莉莎白對於達西先生和韋克翰先生的看法正確嗎?

第十章

P. 52

隔天上午,伊莉莎白收到了一封達西先生寫給她的信。伊莉莎白拆開那封信,開始讀信。

別擔心,小姐。這封信裡並未再提及求婚的事,而是有些事情我要向你解釋。

昨天晚上,你指控我兩項罪名。你先是指責我拆散了賓利先生和令姊的好事。然後你又指責我毀壞了韋克翰先生的大好前程。我希望你讀完這封信之後,能夠弄清楚原委,不要把過錯完全怪罪在我頭上。在解釋時，如果令你感到不高興，我要向你表示歉意。

我看出賓利先生對令姊的愛戀之意。事實上，我從未看見他如此陷入熱戀。我也注意到令姊，看出她並沒有鍾情於賓利的跡象。她陶醉於男方對她的關注，但她對他並沒有真感情，他將因此受到傷害。如果你當真確定她對他的愛意，那麼是我弄錯了。但我要辯解的是，令姊的表現的確不像是陷入戀愛的人。

P. 53

我知道賓利先生並不在意珍缺乏社會地位和財富，但我的擔心還有其他原因。那就是你的母親和三個妹妹欠缺教養，有時候連你的父親也是如此。請原諒我的用辭。這樣得罪你，使我感到痛苦。你和年長的大姊珍展現的舉止，是唯一值得被褒獎的。舞會舉行那天晚上，我決定要拯救我的友人，不讓他締結這門不幸的婚姻。

我後來得知他的妹妹也有同感。在倫敦時，我說服賓利先生，讓他知道，令姊並沒有愛上他，這是唯一能夠阻止他繼續跟令姊見面的辦法。我這樣做，並不覺得自己有什麼不對。我只覺得有件事做得不能讓自己安心，我並沒有把令姊來倫敦的事告訴賓利先生。我知道他還愛著她，所以我不讓他們見面。我這麼做，完全是出於一片好意。我無意傷了令姊的心。

關於韋克翰先生，我要把一切的事實都告訴你。先父去世後，韋克翰先生寫信告訴我，他不想當牧師。他想要研讀法律，我知道他無法成為優秀的牧師，於是同意拿三千鎊給他，讓他能夠學習法律。

P. 54

然而，他不是真的想要學法律。等他把錢揮霍光了，他寫信給我。他告訴我，他下定決心當一名牧師。問我他現在是否能夠取得先父承諾給他的聖職。我拒絕他，他很生我的氣。經過這件事之後，我們便斷了音訊。之後，去年夏天，他又再度進入我的生活。

我得在這裡講一件事，這件事我沒有讓任何人知道。我相信你一定能夠保守這個祕密。去年夏天，我的妹妹喬琪亞安娜愛上了他，他們計畫要一道私奔，當時她只有十五歲。幸好，她把私奔這件事告訴我，所以我阻止了這件事發生。你可以想像當時我的感受。韋克翰先生主要感興趣的，是我妹妹的三千鎊財產。

希望從今以後，你不要再指控我對韋克翰先生的殘酷無情。我知道他很有魅力，所以我不怪你相信他的話，你並不瞭解他真正的為人。

費茲‧威廉上校可以證明信中的內容。

願上帝祝福你
費茲‧威廉‧達西

P. 55

伊莉莎白現在才明白，達西先生為什麼要破壞珍和賓利先生的好事，他並不認為珍愛著賓利先生。他沒有錯，珍並未表露她的感情，夏洛蒂不是也這樣說過？

當她讀著信中對於韋克翰先生的描述時，她感到非常生氣。現在她知道韋克翰先生的不幸，不該怪罪到達西先生身上。

伊莉莎白開始對自己感到慚愧，她大喊道：「我一直表現得這樣盲目、充滿偏見和愚蠢，我一向以為自己有知人之明而感到驕傲，但卻並非如此！」

當她讀到信中提起家人的那一段內容時，她感到慚愧。他描述的內容也合情合理，母親和妹妹的舉止常令她感到困窘。對於她和姊姊所受到的恭維，她表示感謝。她現在看出珍的失望，事實上是來自於家人一手造成的，這真是令她感到沮喪。於是她外出去散步。

她在花園徘徊流連兩個鐘頭，她滿腦子想著信中的內容，後來才返回住處。夏洛蒂立刻告訴她，達西先生前來拜訪，要向她辭行。

接連幾天，伊莉莎白滿腦子想的都是達西先生寫給她的信，她希望能找珍談一談。

談話

- 你覺得把自己的想法告訴他人，是很重要的嗎？
- 你經常談話的對象是誰？

P. 56

最後，她在牧師家的拜訪終於告一個段落，準備返回朗伯恩。

一等她返家後，伊莉莎白便把達西先生向她求婚的事告訴珍，珍感到十分詫異。

「你認為我應該接受他嗎？」伊莉莎白問。

「噢，不，可憐的達西先生！」珍說。

「噢，珍，我真是充滿自大、偏見和愚蠢！」

「你讓達西先生見到了你的偏見真是不幸。」珍說。

「我知道。我待他真的是很無禮。我在這裡有一件事想要聽聽你的意見，我們是否應該把韋克翰先生的事告訴我們的友人？」

「我不認為有這個必要。」珍說。

「我同意。韋克翰先生的民兵團就要移師到布萊頓了，所以他很快就會離開。」伊莉莎白說。

經過這番談話以後，伊莉莎白的心情感到舒坦不少。「我已經把兩個祕密都告訴珍了，但是我不能夠跟她說賓利先生愛著她。這話要由他親口來告訴她。」

現在，她終於見到姊姊，她看得出來珍並不快樂，她還愛著賓利先生。

伊莉莎白返家後，轉眼間已過了一個星期。這是民兵團駐紮在梅利頓的最後一個星期。莉迪亞收到民兵團上校的妻子佛斯特太太邀請她前往布萊頓作客的信，伊莉莎白暗地裡叫父親別讓莉迪亞赴約。

班奈特先生說：「讓她去，佛斯特上校是個明事理的人，不會讓她闖出什麼禍來。」

伊莉莎白不得不接受父親的決定。

第十一章

P. 57

時值夏天，伊莉莎白很期待跟舅舅、舅媽卡帝納先生和卡帝納太太一塊遊覽德比郡。

然而，既然要到德比郡遊覽，就不可能不去想到攀伯里莊園和其主人，達西先生。「我想，一定可以在他不知情的情況下，造訪他的宅邸。」她心想。

旅遊這天終於來到。卡帝納夫婦和伊莉莎白一塊前往他們夫婦倆從前居住過的地方蘭巴頓。伊莉莎白從舅媽那裡得知，攀伯里距離蘭巴頓只有五英里，卡帝納太太想要再次造訪那裡的宅邸。

伊莉莎白並不想去，她很有可能見到達西先生，那該有多尷尬！她決定去求證他會不會在家，所以夜裡就寢前，她便向旅館的女侍打探。

「不，女士，他那個時間並不在家。」女侍說。

這下子伊莉莎白開始對那棟宅邸感到好奇，所以隔天早上，她告訴舅媽她願意去參觀攀伯里。

P. 59

伊莉莎白緊張地望著攀伯里莊園映入眼簾。莊園很壯觀，他們搭乘馬車經過一些時候才穿過一片美麗的樹林。最後，在山丘頂端，伊麗莎白第一次見到面對著山谷的攀伯里。那是一棟巨大的美麗石頭建築，建築後方有一片樹林和山丘。伊莉莎白愛極了

這個景色。

當他們順著山丘而下，朝向宅邸的方向前去時，與屋主相遇的恐懼感又襲上心頭。

「要是女侍弄錯了？」她心想。

他們要求參觀房子，管家同意帶他們參觀。屋內的所有房間都布置得美輪美奐，家飾雅致。

「想不到，我差點成為這棟房子的女主人！」伊莉莎白心想。

她的舅媽叫她看一張畫像。

「畫像中的人是我的主人。」管家說。

「我聽說了很多你家主人的事，他長得很英俊。但是麗茲，你倒說說看，本人跟畫像到底像不像？」卡帝納太太望著畫像說。

「這位年輕的小姐認識達西先生？」管家問。

伊莉莎白漲紅了臉，說道：「點頭之交。」

「你難道不認為他長得很英俊嗎？」

「的確，很英俊。」伊莉莎白說。

P. 60

「你們家主人經常待在攀伯里嗎？」卡帝納先生問。

「他並不常待在這裡，先生，但是他明天會回到攀伯里。」管家回答。

「要是你的主人結了婚，你就會更常見到他。」卡帝納先生說。

「是的，先生，但是我不知道哪家小姐配得上他。」

「這對他來說真是一個恭維。」伊莉莎白說。

「認識他的每個人都會同意我的話。」管家回答。伊莉莎白吃驚地聽著管家接著說道：「我從未聽他說過一句重話，打從他四歲起，我就認識他。」

達西先生是一個脾氣很好的人。伊莉莎白還想要多聽一些，感謝她的舅舅問道：「你運氣真好，碰到了這樣一個好主人。」

「你說的真對，先生，我也知道自己運氣很好。在這個世界上，再也不會碰到一個更好的主人。」

伊莉莎白瞪著眼看著她。「達西先生真是這樣一個人嗎？」她心想。

「有些人說他傲慢，但是他不是這樣的人。」管家繼續往下說：「人們會這樣認為，那是因為他只是不像一般年輕人那般愛說話罷了。」

她的舅媽一邊走，一邊小聲說道：「這番對他的描述，似乎跟你所描述的不大相符。」

「是不相吻合。」伊莉莎白回答。

P. 62

畫室裡陳列了許多家族的畫像，伊莉莎白走進畫室，尋找達西先生的畫像。終於，她找到了達西先生的畫像，只見他臉上的笑容正如她記憶裡的一樣，就跟從前他看著她時的笑容一樣。她在這幅畫像前站立了幾分鐘，想得出神。她認為，他無論是身為一個兄長、房東或是莊主，都操縱著多少人的幸福！他的一雙眼睛在盯著她看，不由得令她想起了他對她的愛意，於是一陣感激之情油然而生。

他們走下樓去，向管家告別，便離開了宅邸。

伊莉莎白

• 你認為伊莉莎白現在內心的感受如何？
• 攀伯里的樣貌是什麼？
• 達西先生如何被描述？

他們穿過花園，走向河邊，伊莉莎白回頭又看了房子一眼。她的舅舅和舅媽也跟著停下腳步，望向房子，正當他們都在凝神觀看時，達西先生突然出現在他們的面前。

他們之間的距離很近，他這樣突然出現，讓人根本來不及閃避。

P. 63

他們四目相接，彼此漲紅了臉。只見他十分吃驚，竟愣在原地動也不動。但不久，他定了定神，跟伊莉莎白說話，語氣就算不十分鎮靜，至少很有禮貌。伊莉莎白不敢抬頭看他的臉，他問候她家人的平安，她簡直不知道該怎麼回答。他也感到十分侷促，一再重複相同的問題。

最後，他好像無話可說，突然告辭離開。

「他長的真是一表人才，身材高挑。」卡帝納太太說，但是伊莉莎白一個字也沒有聽進去，她滿懷著心事，「噢，我為什麼要到這裡來？他為什麼出乎意料提早一天回來？」

他們現在走在河邊一條美麗的小徑上，但是伊莉莎白無心觀看，她的心思全放在達西先生身上。他怎麼看待她，他是否依舊愛著她？

他們繞著莊園抄近路走。他們慢慢地步行，不料又吃了一驚，看見達西先生向他們這邊走來。伊莉莎白決定要表現出鎮靜的模樣。

「你的房子真是漂亮。」她說。接著，她突然想到，她這樣讚美攀伯里，可能會讓人家誤會，便噤口不語。

達西先生開始和卡帝納先生交談，不久就談到釣魚的話題。她聽見達西

先生歡迎她的舅舅隨時都可以來釣魚。

P. 64

「他為何變得如此彬彬有禮？不會是因為我的關係，他不可能還會愛著我。」她心想。

就這樣走了好一會兒，兩位女士在前，兩位男士在後，後來他們改變了位置。達西先生和伊莉莎白並肩而行。兩人沉默半晌後，伊莉莎白先開口說話。

「我事先打聽到你不在家。」她說。

「我有點事要找賬房，所以提早回來。舍妹明天會和我見面。」他繼續往下說：「賓利先生和他的姊妹們也都會來。」

伊莉莎白點點頭表示明白。

「舍妹特別想要認識你。你明天是否肯賞臉來喝茶？」

伊莉莎白受寵若驚。她立刻感覺到，達西小姐之所以想要認識她，無非是出於哥哥的緣故，這就叫她很滿意了。當一行人走到房子前面時，他邀請大家一塊進屋裡坐一會兒，可是遭到客人婉謝。達西先生幫忙兩位女士上了馬車；馬車離開時，伊莉莎白目送他慢慢走進屋裡。

伊莉莎白

• 伊莉莎白現在為什麼感到很滿意？

P. 65

隔天，伊莉莎白和舅媽一塊前往攀伯里，和喬琪亞安娜·達西、賓利小姐一道喝茶。等到客人打算告辭，達西先生送他們上馬車時，賓利小姐趁機批評起伊莉莎白，不過喬琪亞安娜·達西並未答腔。既然哥哥那麼推崇伊莉莎白，他的看法絕不會錯。達西先生回到客廳時，賓利小姐又重複一遍她的批評。

「達西先生，伊莉莎白·班奈特今天上午的臉色真是難看。」她大聲說道。

「我一點都不這麼認為。」達西先生說。

「我記得我們第一次遇見她時，聽人家說她是個美人，我們都覺得很驚訝，你說：『如果她也算是一個美人的話，那麼她的母親也算得上是一個喜劇演員了！』不過，你後來開始認為她很漂亮。」

「話說的不錯，可是那是我剛認識她的時候。這幾個月以來，我已經把她看成是我所認識的女性之中最漂亮的一個。」達西回答。

達西先生

• 達西先生現在的感覺是如何？

第十二章

P. 66

隔天早上，伊莉莎白接到珍的來信。舅舅和舅媽出去散步，她獨自一人讀信。

最親愛的麗茲，我有一件不幸的消息告訴你。莉迪亞跟韋克翰先生私奔了。丹尼先生認為，韋克翰先生不打算跟莉迪亞結婚。佛斯特上校發現他們人在倫敦。請盡快趕回家。父親馬上就要跟佛斯特上校去倫敦，想辦法要找到她。我認為父親需要舅舅的協助。麻煩你請求舅舅前去倫敦。

「舅舅上哪去了？」伊莉莎白失聲喊道，連忙從椅子上跳起來。但她剛走到門口，僕人恰好把門打開，達西先生走了進來。

「對不起，我有要緊事找卡帝納先生。」她說。

「怎麼回事？」達西先生見她臉色蒼白，大聲嚷道。「讓僕人去找卡帝納先生，你身體不舒服，不要自己去。」

P. 67

他說的對，伊莉莎白立刻差遣僕人去找卡帝納夫婦。

「要我給你倒一杯水嗎？」達西先生體貼問她。

「不用，謝謝你。」她回答。說到這裡，她不禁哭了出來，「我剛接到珍寄給我的信，告訴我一個不幸的消息。我的小妹莉迪亞跟韋克翰先生私奔了。她沒錢，也沒有任何一點足以讓他娶她的理由，她這一生都完了。」

「我感到十分抱歉，這真是令人既痛心又吃驚。但是這個消息靠得住嗎？完全靠得住嗎？」達西先生說。

「噢，當然靠得住！他們是星期日晚上從布萊頓私奔的，現在人在倫敦。」

「有沒有什麼辦法把她找回來？」

「我父親到倫敦去了，珍寫信來請求舅舅的幫忙。我希望我們在半個鐘頭之內就能動身。可是毫無辦法，我認為毫無任何辦法可想。」

達西先生在房內來回踱步，陷入沉思默想之中，他緊蹙雙眉，一臉憂愁。

伊莉莎白看到他這副臉，立刻明白，「他現在不會愛我了，尤其是經歷這件事之後。」

而在這樣絕望的時刻，當一切的愛都已落空，她反而感覺到自己此刻是真心真意愛他。

「我真希望自己能做點什麼，任何可能使你感到舒坦一些的事情！」他體貼地說。

P. 68

「謝謝你，請你替我們向達西小姐

道歉。就說我們有要緊事，非得立刻趕回家不可。請把這個不幸的消息盡可能多隱瞞一些時候。」伊莉莎白說。

他立刻答應替她保守祕密，離開前，難過地望著她最後一眼。

「我再也不會見到他了。」伊莉莎白心想。她帶著悔意目送他離開。

卡帝納夫婦回來了，他們在最短的時間裡，向朗伯恩出發。

韋克翰先生

- 韋克翰先生做錯了什麼事？
- 你認為他的行為如何？

第十三章

P. 69

朗伯恩一家人每天都過得十分憂愁。班奈特先生從倫敦返家時，並沒有帶回莉迪亞的任何消息。班奈特先生回來兩天後，他們收到卡帝納先生寄來的信。

班奈特先生說：「他們已經找到莉迪亞和韋克翰先生了，你的舅舅打算安排他們在倫敦結婚，我只要每年給莉迪亞一百鎊津貼。」

「這個消息真是太好了。你回信了沒有？」伊莉莎白問。

「還沒有，可是我立刻就得寫。他們倆非結婚不可。但不知道你的舅舅究竟拿了多少錢出來？」

「錢！什麼意思？」伊莉莎白大聲嚷道。

「我是指沒有一個男人會因為每年區區一百鎊的津貼，而跟莉迪亞結婚。」

「這倒是實話，舅舅一定張羅一筆錢給韋克翰。他真是慷慨又善良。」伊莉莎白說。

「韋克翰先生要是沒拿到一萬鎊就答應娶莉迪亞，那他才是傻子。」班奈特先生說。

「一萬鎊！但我們怎麼還得起他？」

班奈特先生默不作聲。

P. 71

伊莉莎白第一個念頭是，「我為什麼要把莉迪亞私奔的事告訴達西先生

呢？既然莉迪亞馬上就可以結婚了，沒有人會知道那一段私奔的事。」

她心裡難過極了，她心想，「我只想要聽聽他心裡怎麼想的，但是這個機會錯過了。我們之間或許不會再見上一面。我高傲地拒絕了他的求婚，如今卻又滿心期盼他再向我求婚。」

她開始理解到，他無論在哪方面，都是她百分百想要嫁的對象，她心想，「我們會是天作之合的一對。」

幾天之後，莉迪亞帶著新婚的丈夫返家。

一天早晨，他們來到這兒沒有幾天，她對伊莉莎白說：「麗茲，我還沒跟你講過我結婚的情形吧，你難道不會對這場喜事感到好奇嗎？」

「我一點都不感到好奇，我認為這個話題已經談得夠多了。」伊莉莎白回答。

「哎呀！你這個人真奇怪！但是我一定要把經過的情形告訴你。我們是在聖克萊門教堂結婚的，達西先生也來參加婚禮……」

「達西先生！」伊莉莎白大驚失色，把這句話重複了一遍。

「噢，是他！你知道嗎，他陪著韋克翰先生上教堂呢，可是這件事我應該一字不提的，這是個祕密！」

伊莉莎白現在可感到好奇了，達西先生為什麼會去參加莉迪亞的婚禮？於是她連忙提筆寫信給舅媽，想要問個明白。

P. 72

很快，她就接到了回信。

「這場婚禮是達西先生安排的，他替韋克翰先生償還了一切的債務，還替他在軍中買了一個官職。我還以為你知道。」舅媽在信上寫道。

「或許他這樣做是為了我。」伊莉莎白在心裡輕聲說著。

但過了一會兒，她又想到別的方面，她立刻這麼認為：「他不會替一個拒絕他求婚的女人這麼做才對，而且他絕對不會跟韋克翰先生做連襟！」

後悔

- 達西先生的行為表現，顯示他是什麼樣個性的人？
- 伊莉莎白對什麼事感到後悔？
- 你曾經對說過的話或做過的事感到後悔嗎？

第十四章

P. 74

一轉眼，韋克翰先生和莉迪亞離開的日子到了。班奈特太太很捨不得，不過心情很快又轉換過來，因為有一件令人興奮的消息傳來。賓利先生又要回到尼德菲了。

「賓利先生一來，你一定要去拜訪他。」班奈特太太對她的先生説。

「去年你不是承諾説，如果我去拜訪他，他就會挑中我們某一個女兒做妻子，結果卻沒有。我再也不要去拜訪他了。」

「那麼我還是可以請他到家裡吃飯。」班奈特太太説。

「我開始希望他還是不要來的好，老是聽見別人在談論他。」珍對伊莉莎白説。

賓利先生抵達這裡後第三天早上，班奈特太太從窗口看見他騎著馬，朝家裡過來。

她急忙喚女兒們過來瞧瞧。珍坐在桌前不動，但伊莉莎白走到窗邊一窺究竟，只見達西先生也跟他一道來了，於是又走到珍的身邊坐下來。

「媽媽，另外還有一位先生跟他一道來，看樣子是那個身材高挑的傲慢男子。」凱蒂説。

「天呀，不！是達西先生！」班奈特太太説。

珍帶著驚訝的神情望著伊莉莎白，姊妹倆感到不怎麼舒坦，兩人互相同情彼此。

P. 75

對伊莉莎白而言，她現在對於達西先生的愛意，幾乎跟珍對賓利先生的情意一樣深切。她對於達西先生來朗伯恩找她一事，感到十分驚訝，禁不住喜上眉梢。

「他一定對我還存有愛意，但我得先瞧瞧他的舉動，再判斷他對我的感受。」她心想。

她坐下來，專心做針線，努力保持鎮靜。

珍的臉色比平日還要蒼白。兩位賓客到訪的時候，珍滿臉通紅，不過還是從容不迫接待他們。

伊莉莎白瞧了達西先生一眼，只見他看上去一臉嚴肅。賓利先生則是既高興，又扭捏不安。班奈特太太待他禮貌周到，對待達西先生的態度則顯得冷淡。

伊莉莎白對於母親招呼他的冷淡態度，感到困窘又過意不去。母親對於受她寵愛的莉迪亞是因為達西先生的出手相救，才免於身敗名裂一事，完全一無所知。

達西先生問起卡帝納夫婦之後，就沒有再説什麼了。也許是因為他沒有坐在伊莉莎白身邊的緣故，所以他才沉默寡言。

當兩位先生起身告辭時，班奈特太

太邀請他們在朗伯恩吃飯。

P. 76

達西先生的行為令伊莉莎白煩惱，「要是他完全不跟我說話，那他又何必來？他應該是不愛我了。」於是她生起自己的氣來，「有哪個男人會向一個女人求婚兩次，他們太過驕傲，不屑做這種事。我再也不要去想他了。」

偏見

• 誰展現出偏見，如何展現？
• 你是否曾經錯看了別人的個性？

第十五章

P. 77

這次拜訪後，過沒幾天，賓利先生又來訪了，而且只有他一個人來。達西先生已經在當天上午動身前往倫敦。賓利先生留下來吃晚餐，當天晚上向珍求婚。

「噢，麗茲，我真是全天下最幸福的女孩，賓利先生向我求婚。」珍說。

伊莉莎白連忙向她道喜，歡欣之情溢於言表。

賓利先生離開後，班奈特先生連忙轉身對女兒說道：「珍，恭喜你！你可成為最幸福的女人。你們的性格相近，你們遇到事情都會遷就對方，結果事事拿不定主意；你們都那麼好講話，每個僕人都要佔你們便宜；你們都那麼慷慨，最後總是入不敷出。」

「入不敷出！親愛的班奈特先生。」他的太太叫道：「絕不會有這種事，賓利先生每年有四五千鎊收入。」

接著，她又跟她的女兒說：「噢！親愛的珍，我真是太高興了！我就知道你不會白白生得這樣漂亮！」

賓利先生成了每天必訪朗伯恩的賓客，兩個人訂婚的事隱瞞不了多久。班奈特太太便偷偷告訴了菲利浦太太，然後菲利浦太太又把這個消息傳遍梅利頓的街坊鄰居。

「噢，麗茲！但願你也有像這樣的一個男人！」珍說。

P. 79

一天上午，大約是賓利先生和珍訂婚後的一個星期，一輛馬車朝朗伯恩的方向駛來。原來是達西先生的姨媽凱薩琳·德·包爾夫人登門拜訪，她的表情看上去不怎麼高興。她想要私下跟伊莉莎白談話，於是她們便到花園去逛逛。「班奈特小姐，我聽說一個可怕的流言。你跟我的外甥訂親了？」她問。

「我沒聽說過這件事。」伊莉莎白平靜地說。

「你願意答應我永遠不跟他訂婚嗎？」

「我不能答應你。」

「除非你答應我的要求，否則我不走。」凱薩琳夫人說。

「我絕不會答應你的。」

「我知道你的小妹跟人私奔的事。」凱薩琳夫人氣憤地說：「這樣的女孩也配做我外甥的小姨子嗎？韋克翰先生也配跟他成為連襟？攀伯里的名聲可以這樣任人糟蹋嗎？」

「你說的已經夠多了，你把我侮辱得也夠了，你請回吧。」伊莉莎白一邊說，一邊站起身。

凱薩琳夫人氣急敗壞地走到馬車前，匆忙離開。

第二天早上，伊莉莎白看見父親正從書房裡走出來，手裡拿著一封信，說道：「麗茲，我正要找你。我收到一封柯林斯先生寄來的信，使我大吃一驚。」

「他在信中說了什麼？」

「你的女兒伊莉莎白也即將出閣，嫁給國內的一位權貴人士。麗茲，你能猜到他指的人是誰嗎？這個人是達西先生！達西先生這輩子連正眼都沒瞧過你一眼！真的是很滑稽！」

伊莉莎白一點都不覺得滑稽。

第十六章

P. 80

令伊莉莎白感到吃驚的是，凱薩琳夫人來訪後過沒幾天，達西先生便來到朗伯恩拜訪。

賓利先生想要單獨跟珍一塊相處，因此提議大夥出去散步。珍跟賓利先生走在前頭，伊莉莎白和達西先生走在後頭。

她趁這個機會開口說道：「達西先生，我要感謝你對我妹妹莉迪亞的恩情。」

「我沒想到你竟會知道這件事。」達西先生回答，他很吃驚，「我以為我可以信得過卡帝納太太。」

「你不要責怪我的舅媽，這件事是莉迪亞露了口風告訴我的。現在我要代表全家人謝謝你。」伊莉莎白說。

「你的家人不用感謝我，我這麼做是為了你，伊莉莎白。如果你對我的感情還是和四月時一樣，請立刻讓我知道。我依然愛著你，但只要你說句話，我就再也不提這件事。」他回答。

「我的心情已經起了變化。」伊莉莎白覺得有些尷尬地說:「我也愛你。」

達西先生感覺到從來沒有的快樂,他像一個熱戀中的人一樣,表達他內心的感受。

P. 82

愛情

- 是什麼原因使伊麗莎白改變對達西先生的看法?
- 她對達西先生的感覺何時起了變化?

他們自顧往前走,連方向都辨別不清楚。他們有太多心思要想、太多感受要去體會、太多的話要談。

「這都要歸功於凱薩琳夫人。她告訴我,你不肯答應取消這門親事,反而帶給我希望。我知道,如果你不想嫁給我,一定會老實告訴凱薩琳夫人。」達西先生說。

伊莉莎白一面笑,一面回答:「你很瞭解我。」

「我寫給你的信,是否讓你對我產生好感?」達西先生問。

伊莉莎白解釋,讀完信之後,她之前對他的偏見都消除了。

「你給了我一頓教訓。當初,我以為你一定會答應我的求婚。你使我明白我的個性無法使一位值得我的小姐愛戀我。」達西先生說。

「當時你真以為我會接受你?」

P. 83

「沒錯。你一定認為我很自負?我還以為你在期待我來跟你求婚。」

「那天傍晚起,你一定非常痛恨我。」

「痛恨你!一開始我的確很痛恨你,可是過了不久,我的氣就消了。」

「那麼,你對於我擅自前往攀伯里,是否會感到不高興?」伊莉莎白問。

「不,才不會,我只是覺得很驚訝。當然,大概是在看到你之後半個鐘頭內,我又愛上了你。」他回答。

他們就這樣走了好幾英里的路,最後看看錶,才知道應該要回家了。

那天晚上,伊莉莎白把發生的一切都告訴珍。

「你在開玩笑,麗茲!你不可能跟

達西先生訂婚！」

「我說的都是真話。他愛我，我們已經互許終身。」

「噢，麗茲！這不可能是真的。我知道你非常厭惡他。」

「那都是過去的事。」

珍依舊半信半疑。「我的好麗茲，你百分百確定嫁了他會幸福？」

「這一點毫無疑問，我們將會是世界上最幸福的一對。但你高興嗎，珍？」

「當然高興。賓利跟我真是再高興不過了。這件事我們也考慮過，都認為不可能。但你夠愛他嗎？噢，麗茲！沒有愛情，就千萬不能結婚。」

「噢，確實如此！我得說我愛他比愛賓利還要深切。」

「我的好妹妹，請正經一點。你愛他有多久了？」

「我也說不上來。不過我覺得應該是從看到攀伯里那美麗的花園算起。」

「請你正經一點。」珍說。

伊莉莎白很快就讓珍相信了她和達西先生彼此相愛。

「我現在真是太幸福了，因為你將跟我一樣幸福。」珍說。

婚姻

• 珍對婚姻的看法是什麼？
• 你同意她的看法嗎？

第十七章

P. 85

「真令人不敢相信！」第二天早上，班奈特太太站在窗口叫道：「達西先生又跟著親愛的賓利上這兒來了！麗茲，你得再陪他去散散步。」

母親想出這個省事的辦法，令伊莉莎白覺得好笑。

兩位賓客一進門，賓利先生就熱烈地跟她握手，她斷定他一定是知道她與達西先生訂婚的事。他大聲說道：「班奈特太太，這一帶還有什麼別的小徑，可以讓麗茲再去迷路嗎？」

「我建議達西先生、麗茲和凱蒂都上奧克罕山去。這一段長長的山路走起來很不錯的，達西先生還沒見過那兒的風景吧。」班奈特太太說。

「我看山路太長，凱蒂一定吃不消。」賓利先生說。

凱蒂附和道。

達西先生表示非常想到那座山上去看看周圍的風景，伊莉莎白表示要陪同他前往。當她正要上樓去準備時，班奈特太太跟在她後頭說：「麗茲，真是對不起，不過這都是為了珍，你只要隨便敷衍他一下就行了。」

P. 87

班奈特太太

• 班奈特太太能理解伊莉莎白的感受嗎？
• 你的母親是否能理解你的感受？

散步的時候，他們決定要告訴所有人兩個人要結婚的事。

「今天晚上我要去請求你父親同意這門親事。」達西先生說。

「母親那邊由我去說。」伊莉莎白說。

當天晚上，班奈特先生一走進書房，達西先生立刻跟了進去。

伊莉莎白心裡真是焦急到了極點。她坐立難安直到達西先生步出書房，之後，她看到他臉上帶著笑容。

他走到她的身旁，小聲對她說：「你的父親在書房裡等著見你。」

於是她馬上前往書房。她的父親正在書房內來回踱步，愁容滿面。

他說：「麗茲，你不是一向很討厭達西先生，你為什麼會接受他的求婚？」

她告訴父親，她對他的感受已經出現轉變。

「他當然有的是錢，你的華服和馬車都會比珍的更加高貴華麗。難道這樣就會使你覺得幸福嗎？」

P. 88

「除了你認為我對他沒有感情之外，你還有別的反對意見嗎？」伊莉莎白問。

「一點也沒有。我們都知道，他是個傲慢、不易親近的人，不過只要你是真心喜歡他……」

「我是真心喜歡他。」她的眼眶含著淚說：「我愛他。他其實不是一個傲慢無禮的人。事實上，他的心地很善良。你不瞭解他真正的為人。因此請你不要這樣批評他，免得我痛苦。」

班奈特先生

- 達西先生要得到班奈特先生什麼同意？
- 在你的國家仍有這樣的習俗嗎？

她的父親說：「麗茲，我已經同意他提出的請求了。像他這樣的人，我不敢拒絕他任何事。但我瞭解你的個性，麗茲。除非你敬重你的丈夫，否則你不會覺得幸福，我不希望見到你的婚姻不幸福。」

伊莉莎白再次向父親保證她愛達西先生，然後她又把達西先生如何搭救

莉迪亞的事告訴父親。父親聽了大為吃驚。

P. 90

「他替我省了一大筆錢，明天我就向他提出要把錢還給他的事。他會告訴我，他是出於愛你，那麼事情就這樣完了。」

伊莉莎白正要走出書房時，他又說：「如果有其他年輕人要來向瑪麗或凱蒂求婚，帶他們進來。」

晚上，母親進化妝室去的時候，伊莉莎白跟著母親一道去，把這個消息告訴她。

班奈特太太靜靜地坐著。「達西先生！有誰料想得到！每年有一萬鎊收入！我真是樂不可支。他這樣有魅力、英俊和魁梧。我的好麗茲，他在倫敦有一棟大房子！我的三個女兒要出嫁了！我要發狂了！」

伊莉莎白的母親跟著走進她的房間，她的母親大叫道：「麗茲，達西先生愛吃什麼菜？我們明天晚上請他吃晚餐。」

第二天的情形，大出伊莉莎白的意料之外。多虧班奈太太對這個未來的女婿感到敬畏三分，因此對他的高談闊論一點都不敢表示意見。

伊莉莎白看見父親也努力要跟他親近，她也覺得很高興。

第十八章

P. 91

伊莉莎白想要知道達西先生愛上她的經過。

「你是什麼時候發現自己愛上我的？」她問。

他說：「我也說不清楚確切的時間、地點，或是看見你的什麼樣子、聽到你什麼樣的談吐。那是好久以前的事，等我發現自己開始愛上你的時候，已經無法自拔了。」

「你不覺得我漂亮，而且我對你的態度總是十分無禮。你老實告訴我，你是不是愛上我的唐突無禮？」

「我愛慕的是你敏捷的心思。」他

説。

「我想,你應該是受夠了女人老是對你恭維吹捧。我之所以受到你的注意,那是因為我不像她們。一定是這樣錯不了!我這麼一說,倒是替你省去了一番解釋。老實說,你完全沒想到我有什麼確實的長處。但不管是什麼人,戀愛時也都不會去想到這種事情。」

「當初珍在尼德菲莊園生病時,你對她照顧得無微不至。」

「珍真是待我很好!但說老實話,你為什麼又到尼德菲莊園去呢?」

「我告訴自己,我要去瞧瞧珍是不是對賓利先生依然存有愛意,不過我真正的目的是為了看你。」

P.93

「那你為什麼表現出一副神氣的模樣,完全不把我放在心上?」伊莉莎白問。

「因為你板著臉,不發一語,使我不知道要如何跟你攀談。」

「但那是因為我覺得難為情。」伊莉莎白說。

「我也是一樣。倒是凱薩琳夫人給了我希望。」達西先生說。

「凱薩琳夫人真是個大功臣,但你有沒有勇氣把我們要結婚的事告訴她?」伊莉莎白說。

「我一定要告訴她這件事,如果你給我一張信紙,我馬上就寫信給她。」

「要不是我自己有封信要寫,我一定會像另外一位年輕小姐一樣,坐在你身邊,欣賞你工整的字跡。可惜我也得寫封信,把這個消息告訴我的舅媽。」

伊莉莎白的信件內容如下:

我現在是全天下最幸福的女人,我甚至比珍還要幸福。她只是莞爾一笑,我卻是放聲大笑。達西先生也帶著全天下的愛問候你。親愛的舅媽,歡迎你隨時前來攀伯里小住。

你的
伊莉莎白

ANSWER KEY

Before Reading

Pages 8-10

1 a) T   b) F   c) F   d) F   e) T   f) T

2 A. 5   B. 6   C. 1   D. 4   E. 3   F. 2

3
a) When he is with his close friends.
b) He didn't dance with Elizabeth.
c) 2
d) She promises never to dance with Mr. Darcy.
e) Some people believe that he is too proud to talk to people. Some people think he has a right to be proud.

Pages 12-13

5
• witty
• romantic
• charming
• modest
• wealthy

6 a) 7   b) 9   c) 1   d) 8   e) 3
    f) 2   g) 4   h) 6   i) 5

After Reading

Page 95

2 a) F   b) T   c) T   d) F   e) T
    f) F   g) T   h) F   i) T   j) T
    k) F   l) T   m) F   n) T

Pages 96-97

3
a) Miss Bingley
b) Georgiana Darcy
c) Lydia
d) Jane
e) Mr. Darcy
f) Elizabeth

4
a) She didn't like him.
b) He thought that Jane didn't love Mr. Bingley.
c) He was dishonest and he tried to elope with his sister.
d) She refused to tell Lady Catherine de Bourgh that she wouldn't marry him.
e) He thought she didn't love Mr. Darcy and he didn't want her to be unhappy.
f) Mr. Darcy was very wealthy. He had £10,000 a year.

5
Elizabeth Bennet: wild, intelligent
Jane Bennet: easy-going, sweet
Lydia Bennet: giggly, silly
Mr. Darcy: proud, unpleasant
Mr. Bingley: easy-going, friendly, polite
Miss Bingley: fashionable, jealous

Pages 98-99

6
a) Jane: in love
b) Mr. Wickham: charming
c) Miss Bingley: in vain
d) Elizabeth: good judge
e) Mr. Bennet: teased
f) Mrs. Bennet: in awe of Mr. Darcy

8
a) PR
b) PU
c) PR
d) PR
e) PU

Pages 100-101

10 a) 4   b) 1   c) 8   d) 3   e) 2
   f) 6   g) 7   h) 5

12
a) Mr. Darcy
b) Mrs. Bennet
c) Mr. Bennet
d) Jane
e) Elizabeth
f) Mr. Wickham
g) Mr. Bingley

Pages 102-103

15
a) consent
b) rejected
c) insulted
d) elope
e) the perfect match
f) flattered

16 a) 5   b) 6   c) 7   d) 1
   e) 3   f) 2   g) 4

17
a) was covered
b) did not affect
c) had never been
d) had ignored
e) was rejected
f) hadn't contacted, hadn't known

Test

Pages 104-105

1 a) 2   b) 2   c) 1   d) 4

2
a) married
b) admiration
c) criticized
d) fashionable
e) embarrassed

Helbling Fiction   寂天現代文學讀本

1   The Kingdom of the Snow Leopard 雪豹王國

2   The Boy Who Could Fly 飛翔吧，男孩

3   Operation Osprey 魚鷹與男孩

4   Red Water 少年駭客的綠色事件簿

5   Danger in the Sun 憂鬱少年的藍色希臘

6   The Coconut Seller 里約小情歌

7   The Green Room 男孩女孩的夏日劇場學園

8   Mystery at the Mill 英倫女孩站出來

9   The Albatross 信天翁號的獵鷹

國家圖書館出版品預行編目資料

傲慢與偏見 / Jane Austen 著；Elspeth Rawstron
改寫；盧相如 譯. 一初版. 一[臺北市]：寂天文化,
2017.11 面；公分. 中英對照;
譯自：Pride and Prejudice

ISBN 978-986-318-614-4 (平裝附光碟片)

873.57   106016457

原著 _ Jane Austen

改寫 _ Elspeth Rawstron

譯者 _ 盧相如

校對 _ 陳慧莉

編輯 _ 安卡斯

製程管理 _ 洪巧玲

出版者 _ 寂天文化事業股份有限公司

電話 _ +886-2-2365-9739

傳真 _ +886-2-2365-9835

網址 _ www.icosmos.com.tw

讀者服務 _ onlineservice@icosmos.com.tw

出版日期 _ 2017年11月 初版一刷（250101）

郵撥帳號 _ 1998620-0 寂天文化事業股份有限公司